I0604564

THE CASTAWAY AND THE WITCH

PRAISE FOR
IOANNA PAPADOPOULOU

"A haunting and thought-provoking twist on the fairytale narrative. Must we be only what others have foretold and experienced? Or can we make our own stories, flawed and complex as we are ..."

— SHAUNA LAWLESS, AUTHOR OF THE CRITICALLY ACCLAIMED *GAEL SONG* SERIES.

"Captivating from the first page, this is a story about growing up and growing wise, a book-love story as harrowing as it is tender. With a touch of Piranesi, an undercurrent of fairy tales, and an ancestry of Greek myth, *The Castaway and the Witch* is a beautiful, deeply moving book."

— NATALIA THEODORIDOU, NEBULA AND WORLD FANTASY AWARD-WINNING AUTHOR OF *SOUR CHERRY*

"A moving tale of families lost and magic found, an exploration of the power of enchantment and the enchantments of power - with the poetic register of a timeless fable and an island so vivid you'll want to wander its woods (and befriend the animals!)."

— ROSE BIGGIN, AUTHOR OF THE BELLADONNA INVITATION

"*The Castaway and the Witch* is a wild, recursive fable of heartache, transformation, reclamation, and distortion. It casts a magical web that catches you in its unsettling whimsy even as it drags you further into its darker depths."

— T.L. BODINE, AUTHOR OF NEVEREST AND RIVER OF SOULS

"As thoughtful as it is beguiling, set in an island that is both prison and promised sanctuary, Papadopoulou's *The Castaway and the Witch* is one of those stories you'll want to return to again and again. Its true spell is revealed slowly, in layers laden with lost folklore, hidden truths and tragedies —a powerful tale about choosing which parts of the lore to claim as your own, and where to pen a brave new start."

— DANAI CHRISTOPOULOU, AUTHOR OF VILE LADY VILLAINS

THE CASTAWAY AND THE WITCH

IOANNA PAPADOPOULOU

GHOST ORCHID PRESS

The Castaway and the Witch

Copyright © 2025 Ioanna Papadopoulou

First published in Great Britain 2025 by Ghost Orchid Press

This is a work of fiction. Names, characters, places, and incidents either are the product of the author's imagination or are used fictitiously. Any resemblance to actual persons, living or dead, events, or locales is entirely coincidental.

All rights reserved. No part of this production may be reproduced, stored in a retrieval system, or transmitted in any form or by any means, electronic, recording, mechanical, photocopying or otherwise without the prior written permission of the publisher and copyright owner.

ISBN (paperback): 978-1-0685207-5-4

ISBN (e-book): 978-1-0685207-4-7

Cover illustration © Dory Whynot

To my husband,
Thank you for all you give me every day.

AUTHOR'S NOTE & CONTENT WARNINGS

Thank you for picking up *The Castaway and the Witch*! I hope you will enjoy this novella and all the different themes I have tried to incorporate into Nefele's story. I always struggle with finding the right words to market my work because whatever I come up with feels inadequate. For this book, the best I could manage is to describe it as a twisted coming-of-age story, accompanied by a soft enemies-to-lovers storyline. At the same time, this book borrows a lot from literary fiction as it can also be described as cerebral and allegorical. Like most of my recent writing, (I hope) it is a hybrid piece that can be read through different lenses and enjoyed by many readers.

In between the allegorical fantasy elements, you will also find Greece, the culture I grew up in, and perhaps a touch of Scotland, my second home. The novella is heavily influenced by my long-lasting love of mythology, but it can be read outside of that framework. I purposefully resisted any direct references to Greek myths although, in retrospect, I think the novella is partly a reimagining of Circe,

Odysseus and the mythical prison-island Aeaea. Mixed in with the classical elements, you will also find speckles of modern Greece, especially in the inferred family dynamics.

I consider *The Castaway and the Witch* to be a far darker story than my debut novel and for this reason I wanted to give a list of content warnings:

- Death
- Violence
- References to sexual violence
- Child isolation
- Depictions of self-hate
- Identity theft
- Murder
- Forced bodily changes
- Loss of bodily autonomy
- Starvation
- Toxic relationships
- Classism
- Sexism
- Elements of misogyny

CHAPTER ONE

Nefele knew the word dead. Growing up in the countryside, she had seen enough to know the difference between life and death, but the word was difficult to think and harder to accept. She shook her father, but he didn't pay her any attention. No matter how many times she attempted to stir him, his body offered no resistance. She moved his hand, shaking and poking him. Nothing.

The sea surrounded them. She heard it splashing against the boat's wooden hull, but the rocking bounce which she had fallen asleep to had ceased. She managed to roll her father on his back and then rested alongside his body, using his chest as a pillow. She moved his hand over her waist and closed her eyes, waiting in desperate hope to feel his fingers move in soft circles over her skin. She waited for him to crack his eyes open, offer her a playful smile, and for the caressing circles to turn into tickles. She waited for this body, too cold and impossibly still, to act like her father, to prove to her that he was still there with her. She clutched him tightly and pressed her head against his chest, longing to hear something that would give her enough hope to continue.

The waves around them kept softly tapping the boat, and the salty air mixed with her father's sweat. The sun cast upon them a terrible heat, but Nefele was a good daughter to her father. She was his first daughter, his unofficial favourite as her mother had told her in secret for all nine years of her life, and she wasn't going to give up on him. She promised herself she would stay by her father's side forever, waiting for him to return, for the warmth of his hug and the pleasant tenderness of his calloused fingers.

She resisted hunger and thirst, the need to pee. She held onto him. Whenever his limp hand fell off her, she moved it back, reconstructing their previous embrace. Whenever her mind travelled to other thoughts, she forced it back to praying and wishing for her father to return.

Her stomach growled. The sound made her look up at her father's face. She waited for him to offer to feed her, to find a solution to her discomfort. "I am hungry, Daddy," Nefele whispered, wondering if all she needed was to speak to him and he would return to his body. Her voice came out in a painful croak, and she raised her hands to her throat. She didn't realise how dry and itchy it had become. "I am thirsty," she tried again after swallowing her saliva. The words came out easier that time, but neither her hunger nor her thirst pleas brought him back. She laid her head down and went back to hoping and praying, refusing to think of the word dead, even though she knew it.

It was neither hunger nor thirst that convinced her to exit the boat and leave her father's embrace. It was pain. Her skin burnt. She had lain in the sun for too long. She lifted her head and saw that the usually light brown skin on her arms had turned reddish. She remembered this had happened once to Fanouris, her big brother, when he had fallen asleep outside. Their mother had put yogurt all over him to ease the pain, but there was none of that inside the boat. There was nothing but Nefele and her father's body.

The pain wasn't too bad, but it was enough to make her sit up. When her head was above the boat's gunwales, Nefele couldn't help but notice where she was. From one side she faced the same view she had last time her father spoke to her, before she fell asleep. The wide horizon of the sea was speckled with yellow-white glistening spots all over it, sunlight reflected and trapped amid the water. On the other side, just a few strokes distant, she saw a beach. It wasn't a picture-perfect one, like those that made her mother sigh in glee and smile widely. The sand was mixed with rocks and pebbles and bad-smelling seaweed. Not far beyond it stood a row of tall dark trees.

The sight was calming and familiar. Even though they were taller, the patch of trees reminded Nefele of her house. Except that her family's trees hung heavy with fruit and weren't so close together. She closed her eyes and imagined walking in the apple and pear orchard with her brother and sisters. She could taste their juices; she could smell their sweetness. If she was there now, she would turn to Fanouris and make him climb to pick one for each of them. They would sit under the shade and eat together. If she was back home, they would all be together, and she could spend her day picking up flowers to gift her mother, who would have cooked a tasty dinner for the whole family.

With her eyes still closed, Nefele lay back down in the

boat. She rested her head again on her father's chest but didn't move his hand to simulate a hug this time. The pain in her arm increased, becoming a sort of burning itch; she couldn't ignore it, unlike her hunger and thirst.

Eventually, she stood again and climbed out of the boat and stretched her body, slowly rotating limbs which felt as though ants were crawling all over them from the lack of motion. She wiped the dried tears off her face, more an act to give herself courage than anything else, and turned to the sea. She wet her hand and placed it over the red skin, hissing at the initial hurt but relieved at the subsequent cooling.

* * *

When she was older, Nefele regretted not looking at her father's face a bit longer under the bright sun. His features might not have faded from her memory if she had taken the time to gaze upon him. But such were adult thoughts and she was only a nine year old child then.

* * *

She waded through the rocky shore until she stood in front of the first tree, with large leaves, jagged in shape. Their shade was a glorious relief from the sun. She leaned against the closest bark, enjoying more than anything how cool it was. She glanced beyond the first row of plants to see the ground covered in moss and grass. Despite needing the coolness this forest offered, her feet didn't move. No matter how much Nefele wanted to enter this dark, nearly damp place that would offer relief, it evoked an image from a scary picture book. She wanted to return to the boat, to settle again under her father's arm and hide. She would place his hand over her body, hugging her for all eternity, another word Nefele knew but didn't understand. Her parents used to say it to her and her siblings. They would love them for all eternity.

Tears blurred her sight at the thought of that word and how much she wanted to go back home. She was caught between her need for relief from the sun and her hunger and thirst, and her desire to be a good daughter—to not give up on her father and to keep believing he was going to return.

Unable to move, her mind turned to the only people she thought might help her decide between the two desires, her siblings. "Fanouris!" she called for her brother. "Maria! Apollonia!" she cried for her sisters. She sat down next to the closest tree and hugged her legs with her hands, hiding her face between her knees. She pressed her burnt arm against the tree's cool trunk and rested her face against it, realising that one of her cheeks was also burnt. "Mommy. Daddy." She wept the last word because she knew the word dead, even if she didn't want to think it nor accept it for her father.

Determined to feel safe again, she called once more for her siblings. "Fanouris! Maria! Apollonia! Wherever you are, please come out." She used the words from their hide-and-seek game, as if by invoking the power of their play, her present situation could transform into it and all would be well. "I don't want to play anymore."

* * *

It would take years for her to learn that there was no magic she would ever wield that could have equalled that first spell she cast in her childish agony. No other desire was stronger, nor simpler, but still the spell failed.

* * *

A soft tumbling of rocks made her freeze in terror. The sound of something moving amid tall grass made her ears stretch as she was torn between the need to run back to the boat—surely, her father would return to save her in the face of danger—and her knowledge that a sudden movement could be her undoing, as her parents had warned her in case she ever encountered a wild animal. She raised her face slowly from her hands and turned towards the direction of the approaching sound.

Nefele was greeted with the sight of two large dark eyes. She froze and stayed still as those two black orbs examined her.

The creature resembled a horse or a deer, but wasn't either. Its large horns were a different shape, and it was bigger than the largest stag she had ever encountered. The creature's brown face sniffed her, then took on a disgusted look, as if it could smell her sad wretchedness. It shook its head but still approached her. Nefele was torn between her happiness at seeing another living creature—proof she wasn't all alone—and her fear as to what this other being could do to her. Her happiness won. She lifted her hand, and the animal nudged it with its head, giving her permission to pet it. Its hair was longer and thicker than a horse's or deer's and its nose was larger, warm, and comforting to touch. It was so clearly alive that Nefele wanted to weep at how nice it felt to not be alone, even if this creature could very likely be a deer or horse demon, looking like those animals but stronger and scarier.

Letting out a soft chuffing sound from its large nostrils, the creature took a step back. Nefele's hand was left hanging in the air, missing the animal's presence against her skin. It took one more step backwards, retreating further into the dark and cool forest she wanted to be in. Suddenly afraid she would never see it again, that she would be left all alone with her father's body which would never again smile at her, never again hug her or get warm, she stepped inside the forest, following this strange being into the woods.

When she was fully past the first few trees, the animal stopped, allowing Nefele to reach it. It rubbed its head against hers. She pressed her forehead against its large nose and hugged its head. "I am so hungry, so thirsty," she whispered. "So scared." Hot tears flowed down her face, stinging her burnt cheek. In one surprising move, the animal licked her with its long tongue, removing her tears and cooling her skin. It started walking deeper into the forest, and with less fear this time, Nefele followed. The trees got thicker and taller as they walked. Their roots were so large that sometimes it looked like they had grown out of the soil to become new, smaller trees. She clung to her guide, unsettled by the wilderness and unnerved by the lack of sounds but her companion's steps. There was no flapping of birds' wings. No sound of insects. There was a stillness, similar to that of her father's body. All these absences revived her fear, but each time she touched the animal's hair and felt its warm life, the panic eased, and she continued following it until they reached a cave.

She stood staring at the cave's dark mouth and the edgy stones that made it. The stones weren't smooth. They looked like waves made of rock, crashing against each other and frozen in time, as if cursed to stillness in that one moment. She didn't want to enter. Such a place was where monsters lived. It was where animals rested, and if she disturbed them, they would eat her. She turned to leave, to return to the beach and the wide sea horizon, but her feet didn't move.

A hot wave of air made her shiver. Nefele turned to find the large face of the deer-like animal standing behind her. Her hand hovered around its head, before she placed her forehead against its nose and kissed it with her cracked, dry lips. Then the animal surprised her. Instead of walking, it sank to its knees and waited. She didn't know how she understood its meaning, but she climbed on its back, and it lifted and carried her the few steps inside the cave. The moment they were inside, she felt a strong wave of relief. It wasn't really a cave. It was the antechamber to a doorway. She jumped down from the animal's back and turned to it.

"I was silly, scared for no reason after all. Thank you," she said, and caressed its large nose. She reached for the doorhandle and twisted it. The door was stuck. She tried again, pushing with her body weight. It took her three attempts to move the door enough to squeeze inside.

If there was a house, there ought to be a human in it. She could ask them for help to return home. For food and water.

Once inside, she faced a long indoor staircase. She

walked up and reached another door. This one opened without any difficulty, leading to a tall, cylindrical house, smelling of wet mould and wood, and giving off a yeast-like odour.

"Hello?" she asked, and her voice echoed. "Hello!"

She walked around, trying to find clues as to who could be living in this house. The bottom floor was an open round space without dividing walls, with a very high ceiling and panel windows decorated with stained-glass designs of different women. She walked slowly under the colourful lights they cast inside the room until she reached a window covered by a large, dark blue, velvety curtain. She pulled it apart only to be disappointed to see that it was a plain window, without any designs, which illuminated a kitchen-like area beneath it.

Although this window lacked the playful colours the others offered, it was bigger and allowed her to clearly see the room she had entered. She walked slowly around it, examining the objects that occupied the dusty space. It was plain, in contrast with the lush stained-glass designs surrounding it, apart from a brightly yellow velvet couch.

On top of a large wooden table were various bottles and phials. The chairs were filled with mismatching cushions. An empty cauldron sat above the fireplace. Nefele immediately thought the house's owner must be a witch, right out of a fairytale. Her parents used to scold Fanouris whenever he told her and their little sisters witches were real, filling their dreams with monstrous, colourful women. "Just a big pot," she said, renaming the object.

She was back to gazing at the stained-glass windows when she heard glass breaking. It echoed all around the cyclical building. Nefele wasn't alone. She inspected the room and noticed a wooden ladder against a wall. It was in the darkest, least noticeable space of the room, so easily missed. She approached it and saw that there was a gap in the ceiling above.

Determined to find the person who broke the glass, to find help and return home, Nefele climbed the ladder. This led her to a floor filled with books from top to bottom. "Hello!"

She looked back down the ladder, wondering if she ought to return to the main entrance room. Her parents had taught her it was rude to enter people's private spaces uninvited. She contemplated her choices but decided she preferred to break the rule of entering uninvited than to wait. She began walking around the floor. Filled with walls and bookcases, it was the complete opposite of the one below. She found another ladder which took her to a third floor equally filled with books.

* * *

The books were categorised as one massive object, of no use to Nefele at her age then, but their content remade her, forging a new path for her, different from all her own childish dreams and her family's expectations.

* * *

The fourth floor was a bedroom. Light entered it through four round windows, which began on the floor and nearly reached the ceiling. Nefele walked to the closest one and wiped off the dust. A quick downward glance made her head spin. She was so close to the sky, above all the large trees, looking down at their tops and the wide horizon of the sea.

She moved to the other windows and all showed a similar view. This place their boat had reached was an island. A forested island, she realised. Wanting a better view of where she was, she pulled one window open, requiring all her strength because of its weight. She let out a yelp at the cold wind, then paused as the breeze felt wonderful against her burnt skin. She looked down again, and her stomach clenched at the height. She gripped the edge of the window and poked her head out, coming face to face with a bald bird, which stared at her, bored.

She nearly missed the tree bark. It was only the sight of a squirrel travelling upwards that made her realise the house was built inside a tree, or built to look like a tree. She looked ahead again. There was no other land on the horizon. All around the coast were beaches like the one where she had left her father's boat, and then the thick greenery of the forest began. She took a careful step backwards and closed the window. She peered out from each window in turn, noticing from one that there was a patch of pink-leafed trees next to the house, a marked change from the green scenery.

She closed the window and returned her gaze to the room.

"Meow."

She turned and saw a black cat on the bed. Its hair was silky black and its eyes yellow, looking at her in intense curiosity. She moved to sit next to it, but the moment her hand lifted to caress it, the cat ran away.

"I won't hurt you," she promised, and tried to approach the feline again. The cat eyed her and then, in one long stretch, it jumped to the exit and then down to the third floor. Hoping that it would lead her to its owner—and very much desiring to pet it—Nefele chased it. The cat led her all the way down to the ground floor, with its stained-glass windows.

"I am not bad, kitty kitty," she said, but before she had a chance to approach it again, the cat fled to the door. Nefele ran after it, only to find the cat had climbed on top of the animal which had brought her to the treehouse.

"Tell them I am not bad," she asked the deer-like creature.

CHAPTER TWO

Nefele never found another person in the house.

* * *

There were no graves of the previous inhabitants, even Nefele never had one. It was hard but something to accept as part of the Floating Forest's nature. It didn't matter, not really.

* * *

She explored the area around the treehouse which led her to a small vegetable garden, overrun with weeds. She found the pink trees which she recognised as cherries. She found another small corner with berries, and unable to resist her hunger anymore, she picked a few and ate them.

She wiped her mouth with her sleeve, seeing the bright pink-red mark it left. She turned to the large deer-like animal. "Where do you drink water?" She didn't expect an answer, but the animal led her to a small lake within the forest.

* * *

Its existence didn't baffle her then, because she was only nine and she knew little of how water travelled.

* * *

She used her hand as a cup and drank the clear, cool water, and, on impulse, Nefele undressed and entered the lake. It was too cold, and she didn't stay in it for more than a moment, but it felt so pleasant against her burnt skin. When she emerged, she looked at the clear sky as she waited for her skin to dry enough to put her clothes back on. For the first time in hours—possibly thanks to the cold clarity the quick dip gave her—Nefele thought of her father in the boat. How could she be so horrible as to forget his state? The thought translated into guilt which formed tears in her eyes. She resumed her usual position of wrapping her hands around her knees. Had she betrayed him by following the animal napping next to her? Had she given up on him because she had explored the house? Had she been bad?

Unable to take these thoughts, to contemplate the mistake she might have made, Nefele jumped up, scaring the snoring animal next to her. "I have to go," she said as she put on her clothes. Her skin was still glistening with remaining water drops and her clothes became damp as they clung onto her. If she was back there, and she wished and prayed and hoped with all her might, perhaps he would return from the dead. As she thought of it, Nefele knew the fallacy of her mind, but she was determined to not give up on him.

"I have to go back to Daddy," Nefele said, and ran into the forest.

The moment she was under its shade, away from the sun's clarity, her feet paused their running. She concentrated on the lack of sounds, the emptiness of the space, and the absence of other animals. What was it about these trees?

She both sensed and heard the animal walk behind her. She turned, and they stared at each other. Knowing it was silly for a wild animal to understand her, but also unable to move or think of another solution, she asked, "Can you take me to where the boat is? Where you found me? I need to get back to Daddy."

The animal tilted its head slightly as if contemplating her request, judging if it would grant it. Eventually, it went on its knees and Nefele climbed on its back. "You will take me there, right?" she asked again. "Not to the tree house. I want to go to Daddy."

Having no way of knowing if it was granting her request, Nefele closed her eyes and gripped the animal's fur for balance. Her mind travelled to familiar places. Her house. The garden her mother tended. The trees she and Fanouris picked fruit from. Her father's shop. Her school. The square where the shadow puppeteers put on funny shows every summer. The church where she wore her good green dress. The tavern where her daddy took them any time there was cause for celebration.

The more she thought of those places, their sounds, and their smells, the less she felt the world she was in. It was as if she were flowing in that mental world. She was travelling in a different realm, familiar and comforting.

Only when her body left the coolness of the trees and the warmth of the sun made her skin itch again, did the spell break. Before she opened her eyes, she heard the waves of the sea, smelled the seaweed and the salt in the air.

"Thank you," she said, still with her eyes closed, even though she wished they hadn't arrived. The animal sank to its knees again, but she didn't dismount. Her feet touched the sand under them, less warm than when she had first walked on it. She didn't want to open her eyes and face the boat where her father's body was, but not her actual father.

The animal didn't pressure her to get off. Instead, she felt it position itself more comfortably; soon after, it began to snore.

Like when she exited the boat, it was the burning itch that made her open her eyes. The sun was nearly gone, the sky was orange and pink, and the boat was still there. Unable to return to her mental daydreaming, Nefele finally moved away from the animal and slowly approached the wooden boat. She could see the body inside it. She leaned in and touched her father's cheek with her fingers. It was colder than when she had left him.

Instead of climbing inside and resting against his body, Nefele sat outside the boat. She rested her back against the hull, but soon the wooden planks felt like spikes against her back, and she simply lay on the pebble-studded sand around it. That was uncomfortable too, but less so. She pillowed her head on one arm and closed her eyes.

* * *

Nefele didn't know how she slept. Her body hurt less; her skin's burning sensation had turned into more of a permanent itch. When she opened her eyes again, the world was black apart from the silvery shine the moonlight offered. She turned to the boat next to her and looked at the dark, shadowy form inside. Her eyes teared, and for the first time that day, she thought of the word *dead* in relation to her father. There was nothing she could do anymore to bring him back.

"There never was," a part of her mind whispered.

If he had turned into this dark shadow and his body was so cold, there was no chance, no hope left for him to wake up.

She walked to the sea and wet her feet. She wanted to cry, to wail, but she was too afraid to even do that. She was stranded alone on an island surrounded by animals she didn't recognise. She wished she had simply slept next to her father forever. However, her skin hurt and her back ached, reminding her with painful agony that she was still very much alive, and that although she had tried to give up, her mind wouldn't allow it.

* * *

All these were vague thoughts then, muddled together, and made little sense to Nefele. It was years later, when she wrote the experience down, that she clarified them. Such is the nature of memory, always creeping onto the edge of fiction.

* * *

She turned to the forest and was astounded to find the animal still there. It wasn't sleeping anymore but watching her. Its eyes looked red under the moonlight, and it cast a long dark shadow which merged with the darkness of the trees. It looked more like a demon than ever before. Although her every instinct told her not to approach, and memories of Fanouris's scary stories flooded her mind, her feet moved decidedly towards it. Nefele knew this animal, natural or demon, good or bad, real or magic, was the only thing she had left.

"Take me to the house, please," she asked.

Inside the tall treehouse, Nefele climbed to the top floor and then onto the bed. She pulled the covers around her, coughing harshly from the dust which had gathered all over it. She took the second pillow in her arms, hugging it as she did her soft toys, and closed her eyes. No matter how much she tried, sleep evaded her. All over the room, from the big round windows, shadows danced. A creepy whisper stirred through the air inside the room. She was inside, but the outside world remained dark and dangerous. Without an adult to guard her, Nefele knew the tree house couldn't provide much safety. It was simply another environment, with different dangers she needed to learn to survive.

She often went back to the beach and walked all around the island's shores, but the boat with her father's body was never

seen again. Time and knowledge would later give her an explanation. As the Floating Forest changed direction, the boat with her father's body in it simply returned to the sea and his body was consumed by waves. Also, the Floating Forest needed Nefele to stay.

* * *

The second night was easier than the first, and the treehouse soon became her home. Nefele cleaned it to remove as much of the dust as she could, resulting in her going to bed with a sore back and tight muscles. However, that distraction soon stopped. What was the point of doing all that work when she was all alone? She ought to focus only on the things that mattered for her future. Thus, she only cleaned the spaces she occupied, and focused on weeding the small garden, scavenging the island for other plants, fruits, or vegetables she recognised and could replant; and exploring the house.

In the stained-glass room, she found secret doors in the floor, which led to hidden rooms that stank of dead meat, rooms that nauseated her because of their fumes. Then, she discovered a large cellar, filled with dried food, seeds, and crates filled with clothes. In most of the secret rooms, she found more books. The further she explored the house, the more books she discovered. She scanned through some of them, hoping for pictures and stories, but was disappointed to only see black and white words, filled with facts that bored her. She tried again another time and was happy to find books with pressed flowers inside, far more interesting than the black and white of ink on paper. These boring books, filled with words, were the norm though. Unable to do much, she explored them too, but none grabbed her attention. They offered her answers to some questions and eased her living conditions, but she wasn't interested in them. They were tools like everything else in her life, a life which was only focused on getting to the next day and was filled with tasks and endless, aimless walks.

It was three years later that the island brought her close to humans again. She had grown comfortable in the house by then, which had become hers by default. She was twelve years old, and her memory of her old life, full of people and human voices, paled in her mind. From the very beginning her days had been filled with work, fixing things in the house and tending the garden, which left her little time to mourn. By the time she had done everything she thought her mother would expect her to do in the house, she was numb from all feelings. She had got so used to being alone, to speaking aloud to animals and objects, that Nefele doubted she still was the same girl who had stepped onto the island, naïve and hopeful that her father could resurrect himself.

At the cave entrance, Nefele found her oldest island friend and guide sleeping. She had long lost any interest in finding out the animal's species. It simply was her friend, her companion, who taught her to navigate her way inside the island and helped her carry water. Finding out its name would offer her little gain, and she had no time to lose for such pointless tasks.

She caressed its head, kissing its nose and scratching behind its ear. Despite the numbness that had settled over her, Nefele still enjoyed the animal's presence and how strongly and clearly alive it was. She had found more of its kind in the forest, though they never approached her and she didn't risk bothering them.

They were walking under the trees in silence when Nefele came face to face with a man.

His face was full of scars, he was dressed in ragged clothes, and, to Nefele's unaccustomed eyes, he resembled a dangerous pirate plucked out of stories she used to know. Was this her chance to leave this place? The old desire to return home and reunite with her family resurfaced in her. She thought she was done with childish hopes, but there was a man, a human, standing in front of her. Was his presence an answer to an old prayer she had forgotten?

She wanted to speak, to learn who this man was, but she didn't know what to say. It had been too long since she had last spoken to another human being. She wanted to start asking questions, to greet him, but she was frozen still.

The man watched her, and slowly, as if scared of her, fell on his knees.

"It is an honour to meet the famed mistress of the Floating Forest."

Too stunned and suddenly afraid to say anything, she put her hand on the animal and clutched its fur. Her eyes fixed on the man, examining him as a wild creature she barely understood. No words would come out of her mouth. What if this man wasn't her salvation but a dangerous person who would harm her? Was she willing to risk her life or safety for a chance to return home? What if he was cruel? Nefele didn't even know how to find her way back home, anymore.

* * *

Nefele later blessed her indecision and cowardice for staying silent at that first interaction.

* * *

"The tales of your witchcraft are known to all. I am very sorry to have come to your land uninvited. I brought you a gift in gratitude for your hospitality." He placed a book on the ground. Nefele remained silent, not understanding the meaning behind his words or actions. She had no need for another book. She would much rather he gave her anything else, but another thought interrupted her disappointment. Who did he mistake her for?

He lifted his eyes towards her and the moment they met hers, he lowered them quickly. "Will you say something?"

She turned to the animal and lowered her head, kissing it. "You came alone."

She meant to ask that, but the inflection was wrong, muddled in her mind because of fear and anxiety.

"Yes, you are right."

Nefele closed her eyes. "From the large ship with the red sails." She remembered seeing it from her bedroom.

He nodded again. Her animal companion let out a loud noise, and the man cowered lower as Nefele tried to calm it down by caressing it softly and murmuring soft words of love and reassurance.

"Your elk is beautiful."

As he said that, the sound of more steps was heard. More of the creature's species—more elks, which she now knew them as, thanks to the stranger—appeared and stood around her, staring at the man.

He covered his head. "I am sorry. I am sorry. I shouldn't have come. It was a stupid joke. A dare, and I never thought you were real. Some people said you were dead, hadn't been seen for years, but here you are, and look at you—obviously, a witch. Commanding elks and the forest. I shouldn't have come."

His words got tangled, and Nefele started losing his meaning. She stood clutching her animal friend, too afraid to speak or move, too fearful that any further speech or action would shatter his illusion that she was someone to be feared, and then her life would be in danger. Pirates, unlike witches, were real, and did terrible things to those they captured. Her father had told her that.

He was mumbling more and trembling. His gaze never lifted from the ground to look at her face again. His words ran together, becoming more nonsense than apologies and praises to her.

Her mind returned to her original question. Was this her chance to leave the island? Was she willing to follow this man to a ship filled with strangers?

"I am sorry. I am sorry," the man said. No words came out of her throat, none of the questions she wanted to ask; none of the answers she needed were offered in his mutterings. She focused on his words and eventually heard amid his paranoid sounds, "Spare me."

"I spare you," she blurted out. His muttering stopped, and he ran. Even then, as she watched his form vanish amid the trees, she pondered if she wanted to chase after him. She started walking towards him, intending to speak to him, to trust that he could possibly help her and she could have a different life, filled with friends and voices again, not only focused on surviving.

The elk which had protected and guided her let out a wailing sound. The sound stalled her, and she looked at the creature apologetically.

Those extra moments she spent looking at the elk were enough for her to lose the chance to catch up. When she reached the shore, she saw his boat halfway to the ship. She expected to feel anguish or despair at the lost chance. She ought to have scolded herself that she had hesitated and wasted this one opportunity, but instead she felt relief. It felt good not to be tempted with thoughts of a different life, one she wasn't sure she could live anymore.

* * *

Back at her house, Nefele ran up to the bedroom. She saw the large ship with the red sails vanishing away, sealing her future with the island. She turned to the black cat, which was lying on her bed and, years after she had settled in this odd place, Nefele asked herself again: What legacy did it hold? What kind of inheritance was this house? Did she want it? And who had left it to her?

Her brother and sisters flashed in her mind, faded memories of children she no longer knew. Her parents stood with them. Her family, all looking at her, in that space of memory and imagination that her third eye created; she wanted to ask them for help, for direction, like she did as a child. But they were faded and ghostly, losing their substance in her mind day by day, and she no longer was the child they loved.

* * *

When she got older, she was tempted to try her hand at contacting the other world, but she always decided against it. By the time she was an old woman, Nefele determined it was easier to simply wait for death than to blur the lines of this world and the next.

* * *

Nefele didn't hope nor wish for saviours anymore. She knew that like with all her problems, all the difficulties her life held in the island, the answer was hidden amid the dusty books which filled the house to bursting. She climbed down to the third floor and the smell of old paper, mixed with a tint of mould and wood, filled her. She walked through the many layers of books, running her fingers over their spines, gathering dust as she scanned the titles. Many had words she didn't understand, and their topics ranged from history, religion, and art to medicine, potions, and magic. Some were in letters she couldn't read. None of them held any particular use to her, offering no answer to her house's ancestry. She kept walking, and, when she decided there was nothing useful on the third floor, she descended to the second and repeated the act.

Her search led her to a corner bookcase where the books were different from all the others. Without titles. Curious, Nefele picked one and opened it, surprised to see it was handwritten. She flicked through the pages. She picked another of those books and examined it to find it contained a different handwriting. She flicked through another and saw that it was a mixture of another's handwriting and pictures.

More interested in the pictures, Nefele inspected that book further. She nearly missed it because the picture was in black-and-white, but she had spent far too long staring at those stained-glass windows to not recognise the similarities. The picture in the notebook was the same as one of the window designs. It was an early sketch, lacking much of the details the finished product had, but clearly the same woman. She looked at the next page to find notes, giving her the answers to her earlier questions about who the woman was. She flipped through a few more pages and found the same drawing again, only this time with more details. More notes and then a final, clean and clear ink drawing of the woman. She leafed through the rest of the book and found more designs. Some she recognised, while others were left unfinished and abandoned. Sometimes, the author of this book had become so frustrated that they'd crossed off large parts of their notes and drawings, rejecting the idea they worked on.

Growing certain that these notebooks held part of the truth she was seeking, Nefele gathered as many as she could in her arms and went downstairs to the kitchen living space. She pulled the curtains open for light. She sat looking at the designs and began exploring the pages and the pictures, seeing as much as reading the way her house's legacy and story had developed.

It was as if she was reading a story book again, only this

time made for an older reader. The island—called the Floating Forest in the author's homeland—travelled all over the oceans, and within it carried a great witch, its mistress and its prisoner, confined in antiquity by the gods of her time. She had managed to outwit the gods' punishment by forcing the island to travel while she lived on it, allowing her the freedom to roam the world while still captured by the island. Other diaries, written by different hands, suggested it was where witches were made, the origin of magic. In the end, it seemed to not matter for any of the authors of the notebooks what the truth was. Nefele found herself nodding with that final assertion. These were stories too long past.

The recent history of the island and this house was simpler. Like Nefele, all its previous inhabitants had reached it by accident, some completely unaware of its existence, others knowing of it from fairy tales and folklore. They all struggled as she did and they all found the answers they wanted inside the house, exploring and expanding it to pass to the next owner. The stained-glass windows were one such gift for a future owner.

And all of them suggested to go to the third floor, to the fifth bookcase on the left, and on the second shelf find a dark red book called *Goeteia*. They never mentioned what that book contained, what it offered the reader. But they all insisted it was imperative to find it, because only by reading it could one uncover all the secrets of this mystical island.

Nefele didn't need to be told twice. She sprinted up to locate that book. She counted the bookcases and then the shelves, and—pressed tightly amid other tomes—she found the small red book which they all spoke of. It was the size of her palm, so small that she was reminded of her grandfather's prayer book. Excited, Nefele opened it on the first page, only to be unhappily greeted with letters she didn't recognise. She was about to give up when she saw in the space the book had left on the shelf a single sheet of paper. She picked it up and realised that it was a list of dictionaries from the language this book was written in, and various other ones. Her eyes immediately picked up her native tongue, and next to it the location of where she could find the dictionary.

* * *

Like everything else the island offered, this was a struggle too. She thanked the previous women for not making it easier. If one didn't have the will to fight with words, that person would be too dangerous to wield the book's secrets.

CHAPTER THREE

She was sixteen the second time another human reached her island. This time Nefele thought she was prepared to play the role in which the island had cast her. Any desire or thought of leaving had deserted her. The girl who had landed on that shore nearly seven years prior was buried deep inside the one who had assumed the role of the evil witch.

Nefele was with her elks, having learnt to socialise with the whole herd, at the beach. She was gazing at the horizon when a small wooden boat, very much like the one she had arrived in, approached the island. A woman jumped out and started pulling it towards the shore. Nefele stood up but didn't move to help her. She only watched.

"Help!" the woman begged as she pulled the boat. Nefele didn't respond. "Help! Help me!"

Despite her pleas, Nefele remained silent and waited for the woman to reach her. Once the woman managed to get the boat onto the sand, she collapsed, exhausted. Only then, as Nefele listened to her tired, thick, ragged breath, did she approach. Instead of helping her, Nefele looked inside the boat.

The sight of two young children, a boy and a girl, sleeping inside it brought harsh flashes of her first day on the island. It had been so long since she had thought of her father and the state he was in the last time she saw him. They were younger than she was when she had arrived at this place. The oldest couldn't be older than five, and the younger one was still a toddler.

"Oh, hi." She reached her hand into the boat, eager to touch them, remembering her own sisters. She had once been the older sister who fed and changed younger babies, and that part of her rose to the top and guided her hands to reach for a cuddle. But before she could touch them, she felt her hair being pulled, and fell backwards.

It had also been years since she was attacked in any way.

Nefele dimly remembered fighting with Fanouris and Maria. Apollonia was too young. Their fights had been violent but not brutal. They held within them a certain subconscious knowledge that they wouldn't go too far, that the fighting didn't hold inherent danger.

She fell on the sand, shocked at the force, groaning at the sharp pain. But it was a mistake: the witch of the Floating Forest didn't lie down. Nefele jumped back on her feet. Words from all the diaries rang in her mind with all the advice offered from the previous island inhabitants. "Do you know *who* I am?"

The woman shook her head.

"Do you know *where* you are?"

"Somewhere in the North Sea."

Nefele shook her head. "You are standing on the Floating Forest."

The woman's eyes widened, and then she burst out laughing. "That's a stupid myth."

Nefele didn't comment. She turned to look at her elks. Her oldest friend—the male leader as she had learned—walked towards her and she lifted her hand to caress his face. "Am I myth too?"

The woman laughed again. "And who are you, girl? Another castaway?"

Nefele smiled as she had practiced in the mirror. The diaries often spoke of the terrifying smile of the witch. She locked eyes with the woman, noticing the terror and fear in them, and the lines on her face, and the grey in her hair. She was stabbed by a feeling of familiarity as she studied the woman. They had never met, she was certain of that. They couldn't have, because coincidences like that only took place in storybooks, and, no matter how much Nefele liked reading them, she knew real life held no such plot points.

* * *

She pondered over that feeling often in the years to come and decided it was because the woman was like so many desperate women in her old village. She was a memory of the type of woman her mother was, the kind of woman Nefele would have grown to be if it wasn't for the island and all its wonders.

* * *

"I am the mistress of this island, the holder of knowledge, and the witch even the old and powerful gods feared so much they imprisoned me to only be allowed to live here."

The woman's face broke in belief and then disbelief. It was more than that, Nefele thought. It was strength through despair. Whatever she had escaped from, Nefele knew her island's myth was meant to be worse.

"I don't believe you," the mother said.

"Your belief is irrelevant." Nefele tried to keep her voice calm, but her heartbeat rose, and she felt her control of the situation slipping. This wasn't how the stories in the diaries went. There had never been anyone who doubted their identities. If Nefele wanted to keep her island safe and her own, she had to try harder in her impersonation. With no family or skills, where would she end up if she was forced to leave the only place she knew? What would the woman do to her if she realised that Nefele wasn't a mythical being but —as she had accurately guessed—another castaway?

"Then how come you let me breathe? How are you so young? You're supposed to be a monstrous hag."

"I am what I choose to be. You don't understand me." Nefele attempted to bluff her way and lifted her hand, begging more of her elks to come to her rescue. Some answered her plea. "Do you want to see me angry? See what I can do?"

The mother didn't respond. She froze, looking at her children and then back to Nefele.

"Are you not afraid of me?" Nefele pushed.

* * *

This was a mistake she would never repeat again. One she would learn deep into her core.

* * *

The woman's face grew calm, as if she suddenly understood Nefele, and she smiled.

* * *

Nefele used the memory of that smile to perfect her own. It held within it the certainty of power and the wildness of despair.

* * *

The newcomer approached Nefele and shoved her again, making her lose her balance. "You are no witch, girl."

None of the diaries ever spoke of anyone challenging their claims. Or perhaps all who did were killed too quickly to make it into the diary entries. Her elk friends remained still, watching to see what their human would do. Or, Nefele feared, to see who the victor would be and the new owner of the island.

"You are just another castaway."

The way she said those words made Nefele cringe in fear. The way she looked at Nefele convinced her that the mother had seen right through her. "Terrified. How long have you been here, that you devised this story of who you are?"

Only casting real magic could change her mind, and

that skill Nefele had failed to master from the red book. Her small, pitiful attempts resulted in barely visible changes that would neither impress nor scare the woman. There was no way to show she had magic, only to confirm to her she was a weak witch, barely able to cast the simplest spell. Her heart desired to make strong thorns grow and imprison the woman, to lift her in the air as she had seen the bad fairies or witches do in picture books.

Lacking the magical skills, Nefele resolved to use her body, which she knew she could depend on for everything magic hadn't offered. Before the woman had another chance to speak, Nefele lunged at her, shoving her herself. The mother attacked her again and the sound of the two children's crying was heard all around the beach. Annoying, high-pitched noises which brought flashes of Maria and Apollonia to Nefele's mind. The more the children cried, the more the blurred images cleared, filling Nefele with rage for the memories they inspired. She and their mother rolled on the ground, biting, scratching, and pulling each other's hair.

It was her first physical battle since she was a child. It was a battle Nefele found herself quickly losing.

But she had read all the diaries about the previous island witches. She was the only person who knew them as something other than evil hags. The red book said that magic was *desire*. It was the acceptance of one's wants, completely letting go of all inhibitions, all fears, all logic, all emotion. All humans were capable of it, as long as they went into deeper contact with their most basic, raw, animal nature. Whoever the originator of this island was, despite all that was lost about her, this one piece of vital information was clear inside the red book she'd bestowed, the origin and beginning of the library the island carried.

Nefele wanted the island. She wanted her elk friends. She wanted to win. And it had been too long since she had last spent any time with other humans. She couldn't return to a world she didn't understand. She had struggled too much, and she wanted to believe that she had earned it. She could have stayed in that boat, letting the sun cook her skin until she died of hunger and thirst, clinging to her father. Instead, Nefele had been brave and had climbed out.

This was *her* life. This was *her* island. This was all she knew, and she wasn't going to let it go to anyone. None of the earlier inhabitants left it, and Nefele refused to be less than the voices she read inside the diaries, the faces that looked at her from the window panels.

The magic came out of her without words or direction, unlike all the previous times she had tried to cast a spell. The strength was inside her, kicking in a dose of adrenaline. She no longer felt pain from her wounds. She no longer felt her broken nose or the blood running down her face. It felt good. Unlike all her semi-successes before, this spell was pulsing inside her and she knew she had found that animal source the red book talked of.

She let go of all thought of the woman on top of her, erasing her face, her motherhood, her humanity, her entire existence, and clung to that desire to keep what was hers. Nefele evicted any doubts as to whether she deserved the island or whether she was right in being hostile. She even evicted the desire to be the witch. All she left inside her was the simple, clear-cut, and powerful sentiment of "mine".

The punching stopped. Nefele wiped the blood from

her face and stood up. The adrenaline kick faded, and she let out harsh breaths as she rose. She dusted the sand off her clothes as she tried to locate the screaming children's mother. Nefele saw her walking in circles, touching her face. The final remnants of the adrenaline left her, leaving a smug sense of satisfaction for what she had achieved. She was a witch. She was powerful. She could become what all the other women had been. She could be good and generous to those who behaved as she pleased. She could force a punishment upon all the bad ones. Like the original witch, she was made of that something that allowed legends to be born and remoulded the world in her path.

Nefele limped her way towards the mother. Her first thought was that she was hallucinating. The mother's entire face was gone. She had no eyes, no mouth, no nose. But even up close, the sight didn't alter.

"What?" she muttered. She grabbed the woman and held her still to examine where her face had been. There was only smooth skin. Nefele ran her hands over it. The woman's actual skull had changed. Her mouth opened slowly in horror of what she had done. All her earlier bravado gone. She had wanted to show off her power, but left with this empty creature in front of her, Nefele wasn't sure what to do. She was prepared to gloat and send her away or to make the woman her servant for a while. She could envision her hatred- and fear-filled face, but this lack of features she didn't like. She didn't know what to do with her.

Or her crying children in the boat.

"I am sorry," she said to the woman, and then touched the side of her face to find that she had also lost her ears.

Nefele covered her mouth in shock, and studied the still, faceless creature she had forced the woman to become. Her eyes travelled down her body and her hands touched her to check if Nefele saw right. It wasn't only the woman's face she had taken. The woman no longer had breasts.

What else had Nefele taken from her?

Her children screamed and cried for their mother, but, incomplete and inhuman as Nefele had made her, she couldn't hear them.

* * *

Nefele wished she'd had the mercy to kill her then. That would have protected some of her dignity. If only she had put her back in the boat, next to her crying children.

* * *

Unable to face the reality she had conjured, Nefele wanted to flee the beach.

A traitorous voice whispered to her, "Isn't this what you wanted?"

Nefele shook her head again. She had wanted to be strong, to hold power, to truly earn this place, not to wreak havoc thoughtlessly. Not to break things she couldn't put back. Flashes of her parents invaded her mind. Of her siblings. If any of them lived, they would hate her. If they could see her as she was at that moment, they would feel shame. She turned to the children, reminded again that she once was like them. In a boat, without a parent. Knowing that if they ever read the diaries, they would also be able to use magic, Nefele could only brand them as enemies.

"I am sorry," she told them when she approached. She put her hands on the boat and wondered how much they would remember of that day. If she took them with her in the house, how much would they know of what she did to their mother? Could she risk it?

She looked at them, and in her eyes they transformed into herself and her siblings; and still she pushed the boat towards the water, wishing with all her might that they might reach a safer shore, that she was pushing them into a different life, not to a wet death. They screeched louder. Nefele knew the word murder, but she didn't apply it to herself at that moment.

* * *

She regretted that cruelty too. She often wondered if they had drowned. Often feared the island would pass over their watery graves, and their desperate, pitiful ghosts would seek retribution.

* * *

The next morning, she returned to the beach to find her faceless monster still walking in circles. "I am sorry. I didn't know. But you would have killed me." It was an excuse. She knew that as she spoke the words. One that didn't justify anything, though. She could have told the woman the truth. She could have offered hospitality. She could have asked her what she wanted. Instead, Nefele was only focused on making a story to write in the entries, a tale that furthered the legacy she had read about.

She caressed the place where her features once were and hoped that whatever she had made of that woman, she still felt touch. She hoped she was able to feel Nefele's presence and know her old face was engraved in her mind. "I am so sorry."

She wished to turn time back. To restore the woman's face. But nothing changed. Nefele cursed herself because she didn't truly and deeply want to help her.

She took the woman's hand and guided her to the house, accepting the dire responsibility of living with the terrible past she had created for herself. She was a prisoner of this island, like the original witch might have been. She was the horrible witch whom she feared as a child. She had claimed anew the forest, and she saw in her elks' faces that they all truly accepted her as their mistress, the leader of their herd.

CHAPTER FOUR

The monster was obedient and pliant to all of Nefele's directions, despite their lack of ears. They offered no resistance when Nefele settled them in an armchair, folding their arms over their bare chest and sitting still. Many of the diaries she had read warned that no resident witch of the Floating Forest could take a companion. Nefele walked around the kitchen table and grabbed a large knife, readying herself to plunge it into their neck. She didn't dare use magic, not after what she had already done to the former woman with it. Her hands had to be enough. Her mind had to be clear so her hands could be steady and, above all, Nefele needed to be mentally present because this would be a death that would leave a body in her kitchen. It would stain her wood and Nefele would have to scrub it for hours.

She held the knife tightly and approached the monster. They tensed when she was near them, magically attuned to Nefele's presence. They raised their arm and Nefele jumped back, scared of an attack, holding the blade up for protection. The monster didn't stop stretching to find her, not even when their palm touched the knife. Instead, they rose from the armchair, held the knife with both palms, and pulled it, with Nefele holding it tightly, towards them.

Nefele closed her eyes and waited for something to happen, for the violence of the woman the monster once was to reappear, but their palms released the blade and encircled Nefele in a hug. It had been years since she had been embraced and the last person who had held her was dead. Her father, a body she had allowed the island to surrender to the sea instead of taking care of his corpse as a daughter should. The monster pressed their far-too-smooth cheek, empty of all identifying marks, against hers.

When the monster began to move from side to side, rocking both of their bodies, Nefele untangled her own hands, throwing the blade away from both of them, and hugged the monster back. Despite all Nefele had taken from them, their touch was confident, their embrace strong and their warmth addicting. In contrast, Nefele didn't know how to hold them and her fingers clenched around their tattered clothes, ripping them further, but she couldn't stop herself. She tightened her grasp, pressed the monster's genderless body harder against hers, and buried her face against their chest.

The monster kept on hugging her with confidence and patting circle upon circle over her back while Nefele clung on to their body. Memories of her mother resurfaced, which brought smells and sounds with them. "Mom," she whimpered, and the monster tightened their hold over Nefele. When she found the strength to move away, Nefele took the monster's face in her hands, held it tightly, and stared at their featureless skin. "You are welcome here," she announced. The monster mirrored her action and moved their hands to hold Nefele's face the same way. She laughed at the action and moved her head so she could rub her own cheek against their fingers. "You can stay with me."

* * *

Nefele never regretted keeping the monster—who, after that day, she renamed Auntie. Even though the diaries were correct to warn against companions, it wasn't the kind of companion that Auntie was.

* * *

After years of being touch starved, Nefele refused to allow Auntie to ever be too far from her. Auntie, always obedient and attuned to Nefele's needs, never strayed away. They followed, like a young duckling, after the young witch, and their days settled into the same easy and predictable rhythm that Nefele followed before Auntie's arrival. The only difference was that it was two bodies, instead of one, that occupied the large house.

Nefele quickly realised that Auntie, along with their mouth, eyes, nose and ears, had lost their need to eat, drink or sleep. They lay with her in a companion embrace and moved when she moved, to accommodate the witch's position, but were always alert to Nefele's needs.

* * *

Years later, when Nefele had gained more experience with magic, she discovered Auntie's new state of being was a suspended stasis, filled and maintained by Nefele's desire, the same one which had turned Auntie into a genderless, faceless, and will-less monster. Beneath it though, Nefele's desire to hold someone as hers lurked and it had worked its way to keeping Auntie alive.

✳ ✳ ✳

Nefele guided Auntie around the island and was pleased to find the elks welcoming them as caringly as they once had done to her. A young female—a cow as the library books on elks called the females of Nefele's companion species—took a motherly kind of care of Auntie, bringing her own calves to them and gently carrying them on her back.

Whenever thoughts of the woman Auntie once was crossed her mind, Nefele smacked her head to banish them until Auntie, always aware of what she needed, took her in their embrace, easing all of her guilt. The children visited her dreams, crying in their motherless boat while the sea grew harsher and large waves sunk them. She woke up with sobbing gasps and Auntie softly pulled her down, resting her head over their flat and far too smooth chest, and rocked her back to sleep.

Their time together was peaceful and Nefele, already accustomed to forgetting her own past, ignored every tug of conscience. She silenced all her own inner turmoil with the belief that Auntie had only two choices, to live by Nefele's side or to die by Nefele's hand. It would be too evil to kill them—ignoring the important detail that she played the role of the evil witch—and too painful to return to living alone after so many years.

The interval between Auntie's arrival and the third time humans reached her shores lasted only five months. Nefele watched their ship, carried by black sails that immediately made her think of pirates, and saw three boats descend from the ship's sides. She took Auntie's hand and guided them to the ground floor before calling for the leader of the elk gang, her oldest friend on the island.

When he arrived, Nefele pressed her face against his and patted a kiss on the nose. "I saw visitors," she announced to him. The elk tapped his foot on the ground. "Will you escort them to me? Lead them here, to the cave entrance, where I will greet them."

The elk licked her face and then let out a soft growl, which slowly rose until it became a high-pitched scream which he held for a few seconds. Nefele didn't wait to hear any of the other elks respond to their leader's call and retreated inside her house.

"Auntie," she called them. "We have visitors. I will change into the red dress I found in the box last month and then I will welcome them." She began taking her everyday attire off her, throwing each piece of clothing in a heap on the floor. She stopped when she was only wearing her lower underwear and turned to them. "Do you wish to greet them with me?"

As they had no way to reply, Auntie walked to Nefele and touched her cheek. Throughout their five-month cohabitation, the link that connected them had grown stronger and Auntie was able to find Nefele easily. It was only the young witch they could pinpoint though as they often tripped over furniture.

Nefele smiled and turned her face to kiss their open palm. "Don't worry about me, Auntie. I will be fine." They rubbed their fingers over Nefele's lips. "I won't turn them into you, either," she promised. "You will be my only Auntie. Cross my heart." She chuckled and discarded the last piece of her clothing before dashing to the box with the old clothes she had found, taking out the dark red dress and the cool-to-touch satin underwear. She put them on, shivering as they touched her skin, but still smiled at the feeling of the fabric. She placed the dress on the ground and stepped in the middle before lifting it up. She put an arm at a time through the sleeves and began pulling the threads to bind it around her thin form.

Auntie approached her when Nefele reached the upper hooks which she couldn't pull on her own. They ran their fingers on the back of the dress, studying with them how Nefele had looped the threads until they reached the first unbound one. "Could you, please?"

Without needing any further explanation, nor giving any hints as to how they managed to work through the bindings without eyes to see nor ears to listen to directions, Auntie continued dressing Nefele. When they finished, they looped the remaining threads through the hooks again, moving downwards, until there was none left hanging.

Nefele looked at her reflection in the mirror she had brought from the upper floors and examined herself. The dress was at some spots too loose on her but overall, thanks to its adjustable back, it held onto her. She untied her brown hair and ruffled it with her hands before pushing it towards one side, showing off her bare neck.

"Ready," she announced. Hand in hand with Auntie, Nefele walked down the stairs that lead to the entrance of the cave and stood there, as she waited for the visitors.

It didn't take long for her elks to appear, carrying three men on their backs. All of them wore the same kind of clothes, a plain white shirt and dark pants. One of them was younger, closer to her age while the other two were older, closer to the age her father was when he died. The two older men snickered when they saw her. "What's a pretty little miss doing all alone here?" They burst out laughing with each other's words and jumped off the elks. The younger man stayed still, gazing at Nefele, who couldn't stop herself from returning the stare.

"Come and give us a hug, little miss!" one of the two older men said. He opened his arms to welcome her.

Nefele stepped closer walking onto the sunlight, pulling Auntie with her. When Auntie became fully visible, showing their poor empty face, the men's laughter died. The younger man, still on the elk, stared with ever widening eyes at Nefele. She met his gaze but resisted the urge to smile.

"What is this?" the first man asked.

Nefele lifted her arm and made Auntie twirl, showing them off to the sailors. "The last person who came to this island," she explained. "I think we should play a game. I am sure you will know it. It is one of the oldest games, even I played it when I was little, when the world was ruled by different gods."

She let go of Auntie, who mysteriously understood that

they had to release Nefele, and stood still, waiting for her to return and guide them back inside.

"I will chase you. If you manage to get off my island before I catch you, you win. If I catch you, I win." She looked back at Auntie, as if she was hinting at what would happen to them when she caught them.

"Crazy bitch," one of the older sailors muttered and, alongside the other older man, started running before he finished uttering the words. She didn't need to say a word. She didn't need to voice any direct threats or ask any questions. Their faces showed they truly believed her to be the famed evil witch.

Unlike his older companions, the younger sailor was frozen still, his eyes having lost all focus as he stared without seeing Nefele.

"Aren't you going to run?" she asked, secretly panicking that the visit would turn sour, like Auntie's had. None of the diary entries ever spoke of men not running. But they were incomplete windows into the past of the island as Nefele had realised. They never spoke of magic turning humans into monsters—even lovable ones like Auntie— nor of crying children who drowned.

The young sailor startled awake and fell, without any grace, off the elk's back, landing on his bottom.

"I am sorry," he mumbled as he jumped on his feet and, after a quick bow, he ran too.

Nefele sighed in relief when he vanished from her sight. She had no desire to hunt them, all she needed was for them to flee, to spread the word of her story and never return. She contemplated walking—or riding—to the shore, so her figure would be the last image they had of the

Floating Forest, but instead she decided to return to the treehouse.

She offered her hand to Auntie, who took it and followed her inside. Nefele climbed to her bedroom and watched a boat, rowing furiously fast towards the ship, battling against the current.

That night, she settled Auntie in a chair facing her writing desk and Nefele wrote her first diary entry, beginning her story where all the others had as well, when they first set foot on the island. Her previous life held no importance anymore and all her memories of people she had cried for so bitterly all these years ago had faded, turning day by day into blurry images, like drawings on a paper soaked into water. She stopped when her wrist began to ache and went to bed, satisfied with her accomplishment. She had played the role of the evil witch, maintained the illusion of the inhospitable, brimming with magic, prison-island and avoided hurting anyone.

Auntie's arms encircled her and Nefele fell asleep in their embrace.

* * *

The next morning began for Nefele like any other. With Auntie by her side, she walked around the house, prepared food and, at the later hours of the morning, she packed a small basket with a change of clothing, some food and a book, before descending to the antechamber cave. She nearly hopped her way down, eager to even skip to the lake where she bathed. On the last step to the antechamber, she tripped on something and fell forward, bringing Auntie down with her, who was still holding her hand.

She protected her face with her arms to stop her fall as she let out a loud yelp of alarm while the something she had tripped over changed positions and emitted a startled sound. Nefele's basket lay on the cave's ground, with her clothes and food scattered, her book flown to the farther edge of the wall caves, and her towel unfolded next to her. She rose alongside Auntie at the same time as the creature that slept in front of the door.

"I am sorry. I am sorry."

It was the young sailor from the previous day, who was still on her island. Too stunned to speak, Nefele dusted her clothes and offered her hand to Auntie, who took it without any hesitation. She squeezed their hand, gaining strength and confidence by their presence, even though there was nothing they could do to protect either of them. Auntie, despite their importance for offering comforting touch and companionship silences to Nefele, had none of the strength their previous self possessed and would most likely hinder her in whatever fight took place between Nefele and the young sailor.

The young man bowed repeatedly to Nefele. "I am sorry. I know that I lost your game and you have won but I thought if I came to you willingly, if I didn't pose any kind of threat, perhaps you might make it all quick. I am sorry. I am sorry."

Having regained some of her composure, Nefele moved the last few strands of her hair off her face and faced the young sailor. "Why didn't you leave with the others?"

The sailor's face contorted into a grimace of disgust, his

earlier fearful behaviour forgotten, as he spat on the ground and his hands clenched into trembling fists. "They left me, those bastards. They didn't wait for me. I asked them to wait as I tried to swim towards them, but they didn't stop."

"And you returned?" Nefele asked. She looked at Auntie and then back to the sailor. "Instead of allowing yourself to drown, you returned here, to face me?" She examined the area they were in. She held no advantage in the confined space. On the contrary, the young man, clearly the stronger between them, could press her against the wall and strangle her with ease. She would have fewer options to escape.

The young man ran a hand through his hair, dried badly with the sea salt that had soaked in his frizzy locks. He smelled of seaweed and fish, an odour that made Nefele's throat clench as she remembered her father's body smelling similarly as it cooked under the sun and he decomposed while she was in his embrace.

"I didn't think," the sailor admitted. "I just swam back and waited. I hoped someone on the ship would come back for me. And when they left, I was already out and I was cold, and hungry and I didn't know what to do. So, I came here, to wait for you."

He fell on his knees and clasped his hands together, as if praying, and looked at her with pleading eyes. They were green. She couldn't remember having met anyone with eyes like his. She and her siblings had inherited her father's hazel eyes while her mother's were brown. Auntie, when they were a woman, had blue eyes. Nefele couldn't remember what colour her children's eyes were. She shuddered at their thought.

Any memories she still held of her neighbours, classmates, or friends were faded fragments, and held no distinctive features. They were simply shapeless and faceless figures associated with vague stories that she refused to explore.

They were beautiful, his eyes, she decided, not wanting to engage more with her past because of them. He was beautiful, too.

"Why?" she asked, keeping her words simple and rare, because that had worked before. The first time visitors came, when she didn't know who she was meant to impersonate to keep the island to herself.

"I thought, if I made it easier for you, if I didn't try to escape your notice, you might make it all quick. And painless, I dared to hope."

She had to kill him, Nefele thought. She had to. He wasn't like Auntie, a creature that could simply trail after her and hug her while she slept. This man had desires of his own, which meant that if he read her books and learned about magic, like she did, he could cast his own spell. If his desire was stronger than hers, he would turn her into a creature like Auntie, someone to trail after him.

She had to kill him. That was what an evil witch would do. It wouldn't have mattered to the ancient witch, who had been so powerful and so dangerous that her own gods had caged her into an island prison. Nefele trembled at the thought of it though. This, like Auntie's, wouldn't be a clean death, something she would simply find a way to forget.

Like her father. Like Auntie's former children.

She would need to put the blade into his throat and then her own hands would be covered with blood. Nefele knew it would be warm and would splash out in waves of red. The young sailor would spasm in her arms and he would look at her as he died, with those beautiful green eyes that would forever be lost from the world. All because of her. He would die in her embrace or, she might be crueller still, and let him die on the cold ground while she stood next to him. Her fingers would drip his own blood onto him as she waited for him to finally perish.

Then she would either bury him—a tiresome task—or let his body be eaten by the animals in the forest. Although no large carnivores occupied the island, there were mice, the cat, and insects. But Nefele knew that she would need to bury him, to honour in some way her life and understanding of the world from before the island.

"What's your name?" she asked him.

He stopped trembling and kept his gaze downwards, while he still held his hands clasped against his chest. "Simon," he said, "Simon Bank."

"Why did you come to my island?"

He lowered his hands, loosening his interlocked fingers, and stole a glance upwards. When their eyes met, he cast his gaze down again, quickly, like he was a child caught being naughty, who thought they could escape the scolding by playing the ostrich. "Bran and Duff said they would go and see if there was anyone here. They said it might be the famous Floating Island, where the most evil and beautiful witch lived. They said ..." His worlds trailed and he stole another glance. Nefele's face had eased into a more passive expression and Simon held her gaze. He shifted his position and crossed his legs on the floor. "... bad things about you. I didn't agree with them."

His tone implied that these terrible things would be self-explanatory and if Nefele was indeed the ancient woman she posed to be, she suspected they would have been. She kept her tongue leashed, unable to calm her curiosity of the dangers Simon implied. "But why did you come?"

His face contorted into a nearly crying expression but neither a wail nor a tear escaped him. Simon self-soothed himself quickly. "This was my first trip," he admitted. "I was only supposed to do this one, take whatever money I could, and then return home."

Nefele nodded in quiet understanding. Her books often spoke of sailors whose stories began like his. Many of the diaries she had read spoke of such men, who visited the island and how naïve they were. "You wouldn't have returned home," she muttered.

"Why not?" Simon challenged her.

"Because you would have changed too much to be able to return to your former life." She paraphrased something she had read in a diary. "You would have kept on going with them, changing further with each trip, until you would no longer be the son, husband, and father you once were."

Simon's eyes widened. Nefele raised an eyebrow at him. "You really are a witch, aren't you?"

She nodded. She had no choice but to continue telling the story, forging her own incarnation of the witch Simon expected to see. She had no choice but to continue. The allure of the myth was her only protection. "After the baby died, I couldn't stay with her," he admitted. "I don't even know why I am telling you all this. You already know it."

"I know the shape of your story," Nefele said, improvising a lie. "Not the details inside it." Simon nodded, as if he could understand what it meant to hold any kind of magic or have powerful magical vision.

* * *

Nefele never managed to acquire the magical vision. Her desire to forget the world she once lived in, to scrub away from her mind all her memories of the family she once loved so dearly, was too strong to permit such power. It was perhaps the opposite. Forgetting her siblings and her parents so wilfully was a magical act in itself. A spell she cast on her own mind to evade the pain and nostalgia, and to never dare to wish to leave the island.

* * *

"You can tell me. I am the most trustworthy confessor you will ever meet."

His eyes looked at her with confused suspicion, as if he had thought of something unseemly about her. Nefele's fear rose at his gaze. She couldn't allow him any questions, nor any chances to ask about her, to learn the truth. Why? Why? Why?

Why did she say that? Why did she allow him an opening to see her as anything else but the monster? The creature that he needed to bow his beautiful head to and offer his sun-kissed neck so she could give him a quick and clean death.

The image of his blood all over her, holding him in her arms and looking at his green eyes as all life melted away from his gaze, flashed in her mind. Her imagination transformed the image into a different kind of embrace. She held him without blood and his green eyes looked at her without his life slipping away.

Auntie squeezed her hand and the whole scenario vanished.

* * *

She blamed the love stories the library collection held. After Auntie's arrival, Nefele started reading them, feeling flushed at their most sinful descriptions.

* * *

They stared at each other, neither of them flinching for a span of time that felt like aeons to Nefele. It was only Auntie's presence, their continuous and painful grip, that kept Nefele from giving in. Silence had worked before. The instruction in the diaries said to reveal little information because by living on the island, none of them held real names anymore and their identity was made from fairy tales. They had to play along, to not add depth or nuance, because then they would be in a different kind of story, one that could be dissected and manipulated against them.

Nefele didn't understand the analogy, nor the warning behind it, but she trusted the diaries. She would follow their teachings blindly, repeat the same words and keep the act going because that was what the island needed to keep floating away.

Simon broke first. She watched whatever doubts he

might have had because of her words, because of her eager curiosity to take a sip of his life and a break from her loneliness, wash away. "I don't have anything else to say," Simon conceded. "I didn't even love her. She wasn't the prettiest girl I knew, but her smile was sweet. And she loved me. No other girl loved me, and it felt so good to be loved."

"And the baby?" Nefele asked, cursing herself the moment the words slipped out of her mouth.

His lips stretched in a sad smile. The urge to go to him, to touch him, like in the books, was strong but Auntie held her tightly. "He was the most beautiful one. I did truly love him."

Long forgotten rules emerged in Nefele's mind, from that very far away land of her past. "I am sorry for your loss." These were not her words, she thought immediately. These were her parents speaking through her, demanding to act as their daughter for once and stop shaming them with the charade of her new life. Shocked at their interference, and her memory of them, Nefele pulled Auntie closer and dug her nails into their flesh. They didn't complain nor attempt to stop her.

"Thank you," Simon said. He tried to hide his face, but Nefele caught his tears. Her lips moved in discomfort at the sight and the same urge to copy what she had read in the books of love she consumed so desperately the last three months rose. He let out a half-sob, half-chuckle and wiped his face. "Maybe it is best that I am here. That I die now." He nodded and kept wiping the new tears that ran down his face. "You are right. I could never go back. I would sail until I drowned."

He stood up and faced her. Nefele noticed his nose, a

perfect Alexandrian shape, and his lips, which were chapped by thirst and hardship. His eyes were made even more beautiful by his tears.

Fanouris entered her thoughts. It had been years since she had thought of any of her siblings individually, but he appeared fully fleshed to her in that moment. Nefele wasn't sure if that was how her brother had looked or if it was a random face she had named her brother, but he was clear in her mind, grown up, dressed in the same clothes as Simon.

Is he alive? Is he well? Is he loved?

Parasitic and painful thoughts invaded her. Auntie squeezed her but Fanouris persisted.

She had to kill him. She had to follow the path the others had set, keep the story going and make sure the fairy tale never ended. What would an evil witch be outside of it?

But she didn't want to. Nefele didn't want to kill Simon, or anyone else, she realised.

CHAPTER FIVE

"I will decide your fate," she announced, filling the silence that had stretched between them. "Death is a mercy I do not bestow to everyone." She looked at Auntie, as if to indicate that this was one of the fates those who stayed on her island could expect. "I will bring the elks to collect you when I have made my decision. Vanish from my sight."

Simon's gaze snapped into focus, and she feared being revealed to be a fraud, but he stood up and walked away. Nefele froze, waiting for him to vanish from her line of vision. She counted to twenty after he disappeared in case he spied on her, and then she let go of Auntie's hand and went on her knees. She wrapped her arms around her belly. She couldn't allow herself to bend on the cave floor; the island had lost its privacy while Simon walked over it. After a few moments of meditative breathing to collect herself, she threw all her belongings in the basket and dashed up the stairs.

Inside the safety of her house, Nefele panicked. She paced, screamed, and cried. As if an invisible hand grabbed her throat, she gasped for a breath, and a choke escaped her. Could she suffocate from the pain her own body caused her? Her hands trembled and she stumbled each time her knees went weak. She finally settled on the old yellow velvety sofa, which she greatly despised and avoided sitting on. She lay in a foetal position, curling into a ball and burying her face between her knees. She held herself tightly, gently rocking back and forth, which slowly released the dust hidden in the velvet. The itching sensation didn't offer any distraction, instead it brought memories of how her skin had hurt all those years ago, when she had lain inside a boat, her arms holding tightly a corpse for comfort.

She shook her head, not wanting to remember. She squeezed her eyes shut, so tightly that she began seeing colours in the darkness of her closed eyelids and their moving formless shapes filled with faces of her past life. She opened her eyes to dispel them, transforming with that action her vision into a blurry mess, dominated by different streaks of brighter colours and the dark floaters she had begun noticing at the edges of her sight.

They kept her separated from reality as they danced all over, obstructing her vision. Her blindness lasted seconds and with each passing moment, pieces of the world began to become clear again. It was like the jigsaw, those puzzle games she played with her sisters, revealing the bigger picture a piece at a time.

She shifted again on the sofa, lying on her back and staring at the ceiling. It was dusty and filled with cobwebs.

Once Nefele had decided not to spend her days cleaning parts of the house she didn't use, her house had become a cohabitated environment with many small animals, like the spiders above her. Her eyesight slowly returned, and a wave of shame overwhelmed her as she stared at the ceiling, a territory of her house that she had completely abandoned to another species.

The idea struck her, followed by a wave of despair and immense guilt. What if she allowed the same for Simon as she did for the spiders on her ceiling? Until the next humans came and picked him up? She crossed her arms over her chest, finding the position uncomfortable in the too-narrow couch but necessary to formulate a plan. All the things the diaries had taught her dictated that it was the wrong choice, that ensuring she was the only resident of the island was vital.

But, Nefele thought, she hadn't read all the diaries her library held. What if, amid the endless tomes and note-books, she could find at least one example, of one previous resident, who hadn't killed? If there was only one prece-dent, the island would allow her not to kill Simon.

Having a plan, she relaxed, comfortable in the knowl-edge that she had a clear task to complete before making any decisions. Nefele took a few slow breaths and got up from the couch, stretched her arms, and looked around. At first, she missed their absence, nearly forgetting that she wasn't living alone anymore. She paced slightly in the room, a nagging feeling of unease tingling all over her, until she realised Auntie wasn't next to her. She let out a yelp and dashed down the stairs to the cave entrance.

There she found Auntie, standing still, getting wet

from a light rain drizzle, waiting for something to give them purpose and will. Nefele's shame for Auntie was like an old cloak, comfortable and easy to put on.

"Auntie," she called them and raised her hand, palm open and inviting Auntie to allow Nefele to lead them back in the safety of their house. They responded immediately, as if by Nefele's mere presence in their vicinity, Auntie's body sprang into life. They turned and walked towards her, taking her hand and grabbing Nefele in an embrace. Perhaps Auntie held some will, some desire or emotion of their own, buried deep under all the emptiness Nefele had imposed upon them.

* * *

Nefele never learned for certain if Auntie had retained any part of their old personality. Even in her old age, when managing life in the island had turned too painful and too harsh for her, Nefele hoped she hadn't taken it all. But, also, she dreaded that something of the woman Auntie once was had remained, caged in the eternal prison of a body that was not hers anymore.

* * *

"I am sorry, Auntie," she apologised as she hugged them back. "I will never forget you again. That was unacceptable. Please forgive me."

Nefele guided them back into the house and when she closed the door, she put the latch on for the first time since she landed on the island.

They settled on the second floor. Auntie was sat in their usual armchair, their legs crossed and their arms folded neatly into their lap, while Nefele brought all the diaries and began sorting them into two piles. Read and unread.

* * *

It became her life's mission to create the timeline of all the previous inhabitants of the island. Not ~~for people like me~~ for the rest of the world to know, but for the next inhabitants who would find themselves incarnating an ancient evil witch. They deserved to know the real story behind the fairy tale, or so she believed.

* * *

Sorting the diaries she had already found took her a week. During that time, Nefele saw no trace of Simon, who had, like she demanded, vanished from her sight and would only come before her when she called him. She wondered if he would starve to death, and free her from the turmoil of having to decide if she could keep him. On the eighth day she noticed some of her vegetables had been stolen from the garden. Not so many that she wouldn't have to eat but enough to allow the other inhabitant of the island to survive.

She smiled when she saw the freshly snapped branches. Simon had come during the night, when the chance of meeting her was the slightest, and she decided to plant more plants and slowly increase their supply of fruit and vegetables, so they could both feed themselves from the same patch of land. The idea filled her with an uncanny giddiness, a satisfaction that was so foreign she wondered if she had ever experienced such an emotion at all. She shook her head as the mere touches of recollection stirred her thoughts.

She spent the next week going about her daily upkeeping tasks, Auntie always by her side, reading new diaries and moving book by book her currently read pile to the third floor, where she placed them in an orderly manner, half guessing which one took place before another.

Most of her day was spent scanning through the pages of the rest of the diaries, searching for a similar story to the one she was trapped in. Three weeks after Simon arrived, Nefele found the first mention of a witch who was forced to deal with a castaway she couldn't scare away. Their words weren't written inside a notebook, like the others Nefele had found. Instead, it was a series of three pages tucked in between another diary.

On the fifth year since God abandoned me on this island of lonely despair and violence, surrounded by these unnatural deer whose eyes crave for murder and devilish worship, I had my first test. By that time, I had decided I was never going to escape this fraudulent paradise, and I was accepting of my fate; to live and die alone, never again encountering another Godly soul. I had long since forgotten what it was like to care for anything, other than following my most animalistic urges to survive, because I refused to add suicide to my list of sins.

The devil deer, the largest one on the island, who acts as their leader and kept attempting to befriend me once, brought her to me. She was like a nymph—or she appeared that way because I had been alone for years and I was starved for attention and human touch. Her name is Abigail, and she and I became lovers. In this God-forsaken place the rules of society didn't apply to us and, since I had anyway succumbed multiple times to the sins of my own lust, I was too weak to resist her.

She is odd, too, but not in the same way I am. I do not believe she does not enjoy my company, but she does not crave it as I do. If she had arrived here before me, I doubt she would have welcomed me. Abigail helped me find joy and I often wonder if she is real or not, if she is a figment of my lonely mind or a manifestation of the evil power that made this island float around the oceans. It has made its appearance amid all the mythologies of the world that touched the sea. Blessed are those landlocked lands, even if they do not know it.

I was raised on an island myself, on the edge of the world as most people claim, even though I had little knowledge of such things, then. To my ancestors—and some of my contemporaries—the island I live on now was where the first King banished his deplorable first wife, who originated from the earlier settlers. That was before he drowned all the previous inhabitants, cleaning the ground of their magic and allowing us, made from his seed and born from his sisters' wombs, to refill it with our God-fearing and virtuous lives.

I was banished because I couldn't live such a good life.

Abigail once joked that if we searched, we might find the diary of the savage Queen, but I do not touch their words. I fear they will lead me to take on the red book and that will certainly sentence me to an eternal prison, far worse than this earthly one.

The story my grandmother told me was that the King

banished his wife on the Floating Island and her old magic with her. He was bound by marriage to her and couldn't drown her like the rest of her people. He fed her sleeping potions and, during the night, had her rowed to the island, left to live the rest of her days there. When he woke up the next day, the island had disappeared, only to appear again on the last day of his life. My grandmother said that the island reappeared at different times since the first King's death. She didn't know why, only that those who dared to travel towards it never returned.

I was made to row here or drown, forced by my husband and daughters, after they found out I had entered the bed of another, more than once. Like the people from my grandmother's stories, I never returned. I couldn't have, even if I wanted to, as the boat had disappeared after my first night here, and my island, the home of my people, had vanished from the horizon.

Abigail never told me how or why she came here. I only asked her once, to which she shook her head and smiled. She listened to my story, which was a kindness, and soothed me to sleep as I cried, and she whispered that I must forget who I once was and accept my new life. Unlike me, my lover blossoms on the island. Her hair grew wavy, and her skin turned a beautiful darker shade. I lost most of my natural beauty instead. Each day she discovers a treasure inside the treehouse. She wears the beautiful old dresses and parades around me in them, until she pushes me onto the couch and begins to strip. Then we both sigh in pleasure and all our troubles are forgotten. For that, I always smile when she dances around our house in a new garment, because it makes her happy and when she is jolly, she makes me happy.

Our first year was a simple time. She began helping around the house—and eventually took over all the upkeep. Coming from a peasant family she is better equipped to survive on the island, while I taught her to read and write. I did it to teach her to pray with me, to read the books I set for her so she could become a more virtuous woman alongside me, but Abigail soon grew bored of the holy stories. I often woke up alone during the night and found her on the second floor, lying on pillows and reading under a candle's flame. She is possessed by the evil powers of the island, by the spirit of the savage Queen who had been banished here at the beginning of civilisation. She is drowning in her curiosity to find the stories of those other women, other sinful prisoners, who lived on it. She stopped getting up to read them after the first few times I punished her—and I hated seeing her cry once I was done. But she stopped reading them, and that was all that mattered.

So I thought at least. Two days ago, it was revealed that she spends most of her time outside reading. She has befriended the evil deer, whose attention now solely focuses on her, and rides the beast to cool and damp places. Yesterday, I spied on them and saw her lying on the ground, reading the books as she cuddled over the bodies of devils. She hugged and kissed them, like she loved them.

I never felt like she loved me.

I am burning with righteous fury, for I have allowed her to take root here and she has turned into a witch, like the savage Queen of Grandmother's stories. God has sent me this test, I understand. It holds many challenges, but it is my one and only chance of salvation.

I have to kill her and continue living alone. I have to kill her so I can defeat my own lust. I have to kill her because, if I don't, she will eventually read the red book. And then, there will be nothing left of her to save.

Nefele placed the pages on her desk. She crossed her arms, disappointed by their message, and scowled at them. This wasn't the story she craved to read. There was no happy ending within the old witch's words, and no precedent to allow Simon to live. Nefele picked the pages again, scanning her eyes over the handwritten note, as if there was something new she could find, until her eyes settled on the sole mention of the word "witch" which the narrator only wrote once, to refer to Abigail. Although an inhabitant of the island, this woman wasn't the same as Nefele. Killing Abigail wasn't about preserving the myth and securing her ownership of the island but about denying the island its fairy tale.

It didn't count, Nefele decided, as arbitrarily as she had decided many years ago that all she needed to learn came from the diaries and all the decisions she ever made had to reflect the previous owners' choices. She opened the notebook, expecting to see the same handwriting style—calligraphic with the letters all joined together—but instead she faced an uglier kind. She brought the notebook closer, inspecting the immature penmanship and smiled.

My time on the island began before I became the witch. This makes me different than any other I have read about. I was always meant to inherit the island and its animals. Unlike Eleanor, I suit the harsh lifestyle. She did not have to die. I did not want to kill her. But, having read her only diary entry, so tiny and insignificant that it can only be a footnote to my story, I understand now that her life would forever continue to challenge me. She had settled here first and, even though she never wanted to take on the mantle, to relish in the joys this house offered her, she could have thought to banish me and then it would have been a civil war. The animals would have sided with me but the land only understood who stepped on it first.

If only she could have loved the island, like I do. Then we could have stayed friends.

She was not a good friend, thinking low of me because I was not born a lady. But the island is not looking for princesses, unable to work its land, to sweat and bleed on it. The island needs to move and needs to feel safe in the knowledge that its owner will fight for its freedom. Eleanor would have let the whole world conquer it, just so she could avoid the truth.

To the next witch—or the ones after her—Eleanor's story ended when she tried to murder me. She sang words of God and saints, the same ones that I used to hear my brother spit all my life and asked me to understand that I had to stand still and make it easy for her. I had to let her save me. My brother said the same before I ran away.

I swam to the island to escape. I was on the seashore, at the bottom of a cliff, when it appeared. I was a good swimmer. I had to be as I came from a fishing village. I stared at the island, continuously approaching, and I wondered if it would come so close and crash against the cliffs, squeezing me in between. So I swam when the tide was at its calmest. I stopped many times and thought I would drown but I never lost sight of the island.

The animal took me to Eleanor. She looked the part of the witch, better than I did. Her hair had streaks of grey, her skin *was yellow and loose. She was the epitome of a woman in need of help. She reminded me of my unmarried aunt, who used to live with us until my brother became the leader of the household and sent her away. He said she got lost and never came back. I know he didn't want to feed her and left her to die in the wild. He is not a godly man, my brother. I hope, if God does exist, He sends misfortune to him. If He wishes to make a bargain with a witch, He sends him to me. I am learning from the red book everyday and I will soon be ready to face him.*

Eleanor was right. I did not love her. I could have, if she did not think she owned me. If she had let me be myself, I could have loved her, and we could have lived for years together. ~~There is no need to live alone. This island is not a prison, but a sanctuary, for those of us who cannot be in peace amid the rest of the world.~~

Nefele's heart fluttered as she read the scratched-out words. She turned her eyes to the next page, only to find it had been ripped off. She ran her hands over the book spine, feeling the little parts of torn paper; the words she wanted to read were haunting the empty space. This was the validation she needed to allow Simon to keep breathing. She would keep him away from the treehouse, never letting him come near the diaries and the red book. There would be no sighing in pleasure, and she wouldn't parade in pretty dresses before shoving him onto the couch, taking his clothes off him and sitting on his lap. Nefele believed she could practice the necessary self-restraint until another ship arrived, and he escaped with them.

She scanned the rest of the diary, which never again mentioned Eleanor, or any other companion. Abigail scared away most who landed on the island, and she described in detail how she tortured to death two who wouldn't leave, because they were "too much like her brother." Her heart begged her to accept them as enough proof that it would all turn out fine but her mind continued to race with fear.

CHAPTER SIX

She read through all the available diaries in her native language, but Nefele never found another mention of a witch's companion—or any direct act of mercy. All her predecessors had hidden themselves behind the mask of the fairy tale. Some thought of their past life often, not wanting to forget who they were and why they chose to become witches. All arrived on the island when they were grown, and with painful scars upon their souls.

Unwilling to admit defeat and certain that she couldn't kill Simon with her own hands, Nefele pinned her hopes on the rest of the diaries. She gathered all the dictionaries and began the painfully hard task of translation. She began with the six she had found written in the same language as the red book, which she already had some experience with. The task was more difficult than she expected, as she figured out the language held variations and she needed to study hard to begin making sense of each diary.

Six months later, she had only read two of them. Simon had remained out of her sight all this time. She only knew he was alive because some of her produce from the garden kept disappearing overnight once a week. She never saw him when she went to the lake to wash, but she always studied the darkness in between the trees for a glimpse of his eyes before she undressed. She avoided roaming the island, not wanting to chance fate and force her to have to make a decision before she was ready.

When she saw white sails on the horizon, Nefele's heart leapt out of her chest. They could take him. She stared as the winds stopped blowing, forcing the ship to slow down, and waited for boats to be lowered to the sea and for a few sailors to row towards them. It didn't take long for one lone boat to give in to curiosity and she watched it approach. It was just a dark dot, which moved faster and faster as it was caught on the magical currents towards her island.

This time, she wouldn't send the elks, nor would she stand on the shore, waiting for them. Simon would escape the island, and he would narrate her story when he reached humankind, and she could escape the pain of deciding. She leaned against her wall as she stared through her window and wondered how long it would take for Simon to find them and convince them to help him escape.

Not too long after their boat reached her shores, something which Nefele experienced like a tingling over her skin and a slight weight over her chest each time she breathed, a different kind of panic arose. What if he didn't find them? What if he was on the other side of the island, hidden in a burrow he had dug, like a hare, fearing her inevitable decision to seek him out and catch him? She dashed down the stairs, not waiting for Auntie to follow after her, and exited the house. In the cave entrance, she called for her elks.

When her oldest friend appeared, she kissed his nose and caressed his face. "I need your help, my beloved," she asked of him. "Find Simon, the boy who has roamed the island the last few months, and guide him to the newcomers. Let them take him. Let them leave without knowing who truly resides on this island."

Her elk friend eyed her in confusion, seemingly not approving of her choice because it didn't feed the fairy tale. They were locked in a staring match, until eventually the elk let out an odd sound, the closest to a sigh Nefele had ever heard come out of his body, and turned around. She went back inside, making sure to lower the door latch, and climbed back to her bedroom, to the highest vantage point. Auntie was sitting on the bed, followed by the bad odour that had begun to surround them. Their clothes needed to be washed, as did their body, but Nefele feared seeing what was underneath. She preferred the bad smell and the muddy sheets over facing the full extent of Nefele's magical damage.

The boat reappeared on the sea during sunset, rowing back to the ship. Soon, the winds would blow them towards the opposite direction of the island, which would float away, vanishing like a ghost amid the waves.

Nefele slept soundly that night and went dancing around the island the next morning. She bathed without looking behind her shoulder for spying eyes and she entered and exited her house without any fear. The female elk cow, who was loving and kind to Auntie, guided them in the water, surrounded by her children, thus allowing Auntie to be somewhat cleaner. That night, Nefele decided to become a little braver and washed Auntie's feet with a towel before sleeping together, cuddling in the safety that Simon's green eyes would never gaze upon either of them.

* * *

She dreamed of those eyes though.

* * *

Simon's escape felt like a certainty, even though Nefele wasn't there to watch him leave. Her whole body floated over the grass and she was free to live on her island, rejoicing in the freedom she had lost while Simon resided on it. She hoped it would be months, if not years, since another person appeared, and by then, Nefele would meet them at the shore, scaring them away without the chance of one of them being stranded behind. She abandoned her translating, no longer needing a time sensitive answer, and picked up other books.

When she saw that someone—or some animal, she tried to reassure herself—had taken some of the produce from her garden, her mind blanked of all thoughts. She tried to convince herself that it was a hungry animal instead of Simon. She tried to ignore the voice in her head which whispered that only one living being had ever stolen from her. The animals would leave traces of the food they had eaten, or they would be worms that would get to some fruit and consume them as they hang from the branches.

She stared at the empty branches, feeling smaller than ever before, while the island grew exponentially bigger around her. She dared a look around her, wondering again if Simon's green eyes hid in between the leaves, the perfect camouflage. She let out a silent scream, terrified of what Simon would think if he heard her, and pressed her hands onto the ground.

After the incident with Auntie, Nefele's attempts with magic held within them an internal gulp, which she could only describe as a nonphysical hiccup. It was uncomfortable and, if she forced herself to perform magic too often, painful. She avoided thinking of the encounter and the beach. The children's cries were too loud and the memory of who Auntie was before they become her beloved companion was a scattered sequence of details, all placed in the wrong order and without any meaning behind them.

She remembered it after she finished her silent wail. Her lack of noise had turned into a presence of magic, one that pulled all her disparate images of Auntie and their previous self together and reminded Nefele of how their transformation had happened. It moved smoothly all over her, echoing her clear and deeply honest desire of "I want this to be over!". There was no hiccup-like jolt, no painful or uncomfortable sensation. Only a slight feeling of warmth, as the adrenaline rose.

Her facial muscles spasmed as her mouth opened and closed, her lips stretched into half smiles that she dropped when she felt them. Her lungs contracted, as if she was going to cry—or laugh—but no sound came out. Her hands moved to her face, feeling her lips, which were elongated but not smiling, and traced her teeth, before moving up to her hair, grabbing a fistful and pulling it.

She tried to make a sound. To scream. To laugh. But there was nothing left inside her.

Nefele jumped on her feet and ran back to her house, not bothering to lock her door. There was no reason to, anymore. She had killed him. She had tried so hard to keep him alive, and she had failed. Auntie was sitting on the yellow sofa but Nefele dashed past them, running to her bed on the top floor.

She curled into a ball, under her covers, holding onto her pillow tightly, and bit its corner with all her strength. If she was biting flesh, Nefele knew she would tear the skin apart.

She gathered the covers tighter around her body, cocooning herself as if there were any kind of incubation that could change her back into a girl again. She had lost both her own human nature and the fairy tale. What she lived was a nightmare, filled with ugly details, reminiscent of the world her history books detailed and monstrous humans like her. It made little difference that she had killed with magic instead of a knife.

When her traitorous and amorous mind whispered that in folk stories the witches either killed or died, Nefele dug her nails into her cheek. The pain was the most welcome feeling, releasing the tension inside her body. She pressed her nails deeper inside her flesh, feeling blood roll down to her chin, like red tears, and then drop onto her sheets, dirtying them. She fell asleep with the feeling of pain, clarifying her guilt and her need for punishment.

She woke up again when the sun began to descend. It hadn't been a lot of hours as their days were significantly shorter than before Simon had arrived. Nefele woke up alone in bed. Auntie hadn't come to her rescue, to clean her cheeks from the blood and comfort her with a merciful hug. She smiled as she stretched her hand over the empty side of the bed. Her fingers had dried spots of blood and her fingernails were dark underneath, filled with mud and pieces of her own skin.

"I deserve this," she whispered, before falling asleep again.

* * *

The next five days Nefele stayed in her bed, only getting up to relieve herself and attempt to eat, before falling back asleep. She dreamed of her mother and father, wearing faces she couldn't ascertain if they were theirs or taken from one of the pictures in her books. Neither of them could find the strength to look at her. Fanouris shoved her to the ground and kicked her, calling her names and throwing insults, while her little sisters took Auntie's hands and guided them away. They would turn their heads, looking like wise-beyond-their-years children, and whisper, "You don't deserve them."

She couldn't even nod her agreement, because of Fanouris's kicks. The ground beneath her would take human form, growing hands which encircled her, holding her tightly. They protected her from her brother's violence but they also dragged her down, burying her alive. The ground human was a man and when she looked into his face, she was greeted with familiar green eyes.

Simon entered her thoughts when she was awake. She feared walking around the island, because she didn't know what she would encounter. Would there be another crea-ture like Auntie roaming? Would she find a simple corpse?

Would she find a different kind of creature? She despised her cowardice. What kind of cruel creator didn't even have the courage to face the fruit of their labours?

She finally decided that Simon occupied the ground. She had cast her magic while she pressed her hands against it, and he appeared as a manifestation of it in her dreams.

Nefele had stopped counting the days when Auntie finally came upstairs. They weren't gentle when they woke her. They pulled the covers from her body, grabbed her torso, and pulled her off the bed. She didn't immediately wake up. Her dreams were filled with violence and pain, and she supposed her reality ought to be the same. Auntie let her body fall on the floor, which was enough of a shock to force Nefele into consciousness.

"Auntie?" she whispered as she rubbed her eyes, removing the accumulated eye-gum.

Auntie squatted and pulled her upwards, forcing her to stand. They pushed her towards the ladder that allowed them to exit and enter the bedroom. "I don't want to go down, Auntie." She tried to return to bed, but Auntie, despite their lack of eyes, grabbed her and pushed towards the ladder again.

"I said, I don't want to, Auntie," Nefele snapped.

Auntie slapped her face.

Her cheek, filled with scabbed nail scratches, stung. The pain quickly turned into a burning sensation and Nefele shed a few silent tears as she stared at her companion, who, ever since they had been welcomed into her home, had only been kind and warm. Her ire rose quickly and accusations formed in her tongue. But they couldn't roll off it. Auntie deserved to hurt her.

If Auntie didn't hurt her, who else would?

"I am sorry, Auntie," she whispered. She turned her head, offering her other cheek.

They didn't hit her a second time. They moved closer, took her hand, and pulled her to the ladder. Nefele sighed in defeat and climbed downwards, with Auntie following.

When they reached the first floor, Auntie took her hand and guided her to the closest box of garments and tried to take off her clothes. "I don't want to," she protested but Auntie's hands turned forceful as they tore her existing shirt off her.

There was a loud knock on her door, which startled her. "Open up, witch!"

It was a male voice. She recognised it, mostly because she had heard so few voices in years. "Just a minute," she called, without considering that he wasn't her neighbour but a dangerous enemy, who she had hurt with her magic. Suddenly very aware of her upper bareness, she roamed the box. Not having enough time to put on any dress properly, Nefele searched for a shirt and found a plain white one, clearly for a man and too big for her. She slipped her hands through the sleeves and buttoned it quickly.

She moved to the door and her fingers hovered over the handle, because she didn't know how Simon would look behind it. He had retained his mouth and voice, something that Nefele was immensely relieved for, but whatever creature stood behind that door, it wasn't the young man she had last seen. The thought of never opening the door was too tempting but she didn't get enough time to consider it because he banged on it again. It shook from his force, raising dust from the ground and making Nefele step backwards.

The person Auntie used to be had hurt her. Nefele remembered the pain of her cracked bones, the flashes of memories it sparked of childhood fights, filled with equivalent acts but devoid of the adult desire to destroy. Her dream brother took the role of punisher, shoving her onto the ground, until Simon, in the form of humanoid mud, pulled her inside him. Whether she opened or not the door, Nefele realised she couldn't avoid being broken.

Her hand moved to the door and twisted the handle, opening it. She hadn't locked it. All that had kept Simon out of the treehouse was his own fear of her, which, she finally admitted, was fair.

Unlike their last meeting, he didn't lower his gaze. His beautifully bright green eyes stared at her as he came into fuller view, and she was struck with an inordinate amount of gratitude that they had remained present on his face. With great self-restraint, she examined the rest of him, taking all the information his physical appearance gave her. She noticed his tiredness and sensed his despair. The man in front of her was exhausted, both mentally and physically, but he appeared to have remained intact.

"I want it all to be over," he said, voicing her own desire from a few days before, the one that had sparked her magic and driven her to self-hating despair.

"Why didn't you go with the men that arrived on the island a few days ago?" she questioned him. "I sent my elks to guide you to them."

His eyes widened and then his mouth stretched into a smile, far too ugly for his face. Simon let out a harsh choking sound, instead of the laughter that his expression suggested. "You know nothing of the world, do you?" Nefele didn't know how to respond to his words, so she remained silent, waiting for more from him. "I just couldn't go with them," Simon said, and exhaled. His shoulders slumped and his body hunched, appearing older in the span of half a breath.

She could have questioned him—and should have—to continue playing the role but instead Nefele accepted his decision and stepped aside. "Come in," she invited him. He walked slowly inside the tree house, and she studied how his gaze, despite the weariness, sharpened as he took in her home. A faint smile formed on both of their lips when he looked at the stained-glass windows. She trailed after him, feeling like she was following her own self, from when she was simply Nefele.

He tensed when he noticed Auntie, standing amid the strewn clothes and the half-empty box. "This is Auntie," she introduced them. "Auntie, this is Simon."

She stepped between them, shielding Auntie from Simon's scared face, who only saw them as a monster, but also Simon from Auntie, because she understood why their sight filled him with such unease. "Do you want to take a seat?" she suggested and pointed towards the ugly yellow couch. He nodded and did as she asked. Nefele turned to Auntie and held their hand. In that silent, magical way, that held their lives linked, Auntie turned around and went to stand in one of the far corners of the ground floor. Simon spied on them from the corner of his eyes, but he appeared more relaxed when they were banished from his direct line of vision.

Nefele approached him, unsure what she should do next. A part of her craved to touch him and make sure that there wasn't any part of him missing beneath the clothes and another urged her to put as much distance between them as possible. Something critical was going to happen and she understood that the responsibility to guide both to that moment was hers.

For this painful pause of life to end.

She took a step closer to him but froze before she could make the second one, because he looked at her and was so real and so pained. A pang of guilt crushed her. A crippling weight settled onto her chest and she thought she would faint from the pain and the lack of breathing. "I," she stammered, trying to speak and breathe, but both were impossible. Her mind blanked and her body was ready to crumble.

This was an end, too, she thought. If she collapsed, he would need to decide how to proceed and what would happen between them. He could kill her and keep the house, or help her and hold her through the debt. Either way, Nefele would escape the decision.

"I am hungry," Simon said. He didn't speak loudly but he enunciated the words strongly and she heard him beneath the loud thumping in her ears.

"Yes," she said, the pain lifted as her mind settled on a simple task to complete. "I have food."

She tore a large piece of the stale potato bread she had made days ago and filled his plate with some of the dried meat she had taken out of the cellar, where most of her food supplies originated. She filled a cup with clean water, which she had boiled the same day she made the bread.

Nefele nearly failed to deliver them to him, but he

reached for them, and she handed them over. They sat together on the yellow couch, each to one end, while he ate in silence. It had been years since she had ever played any kind of host. She vaguely remembered her mother having people over. Only that there was constant talking. "I can cook you something warm, if you don't like this."

The silence returned between them while he chewed and stared at her. The longer he looked, the smaller Nefele felt, like in the dream, when his mud body absorbed her until there was nothing left of her. He finally shook his head and returned his attention to the bread. "I have only been eating raw fruit and vegetables all these months. This tastes beautiful. Thank you."

"I didn't want to make it obvious," she apologised.

"What?"

"The additional vegetable and fruit for you that I cultivated the last few months. I didn't want you to think I was kind. That's why I never left any other food out for you."

He choked on the bread and coughed loudly, spitting bits out. Nefele remained still as she watched him struggle. His airways eventually cleared and he took the cup and drank. "I didn't realise you knew what I was doing. I tried not to leave any evidence."

She smiled. "This island is an extension of me. I know a lot of what happens on it." Nefele hated herself for these words, because they were part of the role of the witch and she didn't want to play it anymore.

Simon eyed her with suspicion, as if he recognised the dichotomy between Nefele and the witch persona she put on, the lines between them becoming clearer with every word she uttered. "I am really tired," he admitted, putting the half-eaten food on the little coffee table.

"Go upstairs," Nefele offered. "To the fourth floor, that's the bedroom. Go and sleep there."

"A bed?" he muttered and she recognised his hunger for it.

"A bed. I can go and change the sheets, so it will be clean."

"I slept on the ground for months, using piles of leaves for pillows. A dirty bed sounds like heaven," he replied.

The crushing weight on her chest returned, and she named the feeling guilt. Her inability to play the witch had led to his suspended state of life all these months. Her indecision to take charge and resolve the situation prolonged his hardship until, finally, she had done something to him with her magic, even if she couldn't see it yet.

"Go to bed then," she urged him, repeating her suggestion.

He stood up and followed her to the ladder. He began climbing it but when he was halfway he looked down towards her. "Will you be here when I wake up?"

She nodded.

"That's good."

* * *

Many years later, when Nefele was an old woman, she admitted ~~to me~~ *that offering her bed was the right choice, and it marked a momentous change in the history of the Floating Forest.*

CHAPTER SEVEN

He slept through the entire day and night. Nefele waited on the ground floor, sometimes sitting on a kitchen chair and other times pacing around the empty space, but her eyes always moved to the stained-glass windows, illuminated by the moonlight. Their colours lacked the vibrancy the direct sunlight offered them, but Nefele often thought that their truer nature was shown under the moon and stars. The witches' faces appeared sadder, less glorious in their supreme height, and more like trapped souls in their individual panels. She had found the artist's diary—it was the first one she read—who wrote with painful detail how she chose which previous witch to illustrate for her windows. Unlike these older witches, the artist witch appeared to have lived through an easy tenure, with years-long stretches of solitude interrupted by easy-to-scare visitors. That peace had allowed for her art.

* * *

Nefele eventually found all but one of their diaries. Most were tattered and in pieces, some of the oldest residents of the island, written in mostly forgotten languages. Like every treasure and joy the island offered, their stories demanded hard work to be unearthed. Nothing came easy to any of the witches. They were, after all, prisoners, like the very first, now nameless, witch who had started it all.

* * *

She heard Simon when he descended the stairs, as Nefele had been listening as he took a few minutes to look at her library before he climbed down the final ladder. She didn't mind, nor blame his curiosity. His life on the island since their second meeting had been harsh, empty survivalism, devoid of any kind of entertainment, or intellectual stimulation. His perusal allowed her time to reheat the vegetable soup she had prepared for him. She had wanted to add crab shells inside it, to boost the flavour, but Nefele feared that he might wake up while she was gone and wished to keep her promise.

She tore a large chunk of the new potato bread she had baked, which had come out stodgier than she would have liked, and placed it on the table, next to the bowl of soup she had laid out for him.

"I have made you soup," she said, unsure of what else she could say but wanting him to feel safe. Before he slept, his hunger had been the bridge of their communication and Nefele wished, after months of lack of nutrition and so many hours of sleeping, that Simon would remain hungry enough to lower his guard in exchange for food.

Her wish was fulfilled. Simon's uneasiness lessened at the smell of food and he approached the kitchen table. A strange feeling of relief flowed through her as Simon ate the bread without complaint or any sign of criticism. He looked around the kitchen, taking in the space anew after his sleep. "Where is ...?" he trailed.

"Auntie?" Nefele asked. He nodded. "They are sitting at the third floor."

He didn't ask for more information and Nefele didn't provide him with any further words. She watched him eat fast, swallowing the soft vegetables, before taking another bite of the bread. When he finished, Nefele brought him water and gathered the plates back to the kitchen counter. "I have fruit jam, if you want."

He shook his head but didn't say anything else. Nefele returned to the table and a tension-free silence reigned between them. Various questions rose to her lips but she kept them to herself. After so many years of pretending to be the mythical witch, of assimilating the tale to always appear in control and otherworldly, she struggled to shed the façade and act in a way that offered any kind of power leverage against her. Even at that moment, after she had fed him and allowed him into her bed, Nefele couldn't ignore the self-preservation instinct that kicked in and warned her to not lower her guard completely.

She kept her gazed fixed on Simon, watching him stare at his hands until he eventually lifted his eyes and stared back at her. Under the sunlight and after some rest, his eyes had regained their brightness but, within them, Nefele still discerned his exhaustion. She had read that all problems eventually reached their boiling point, forcing those involved to act. This was that point for them.

Something had to change for both of their lives to move on, whether that was to move on in life or beyond it for one of them.

"Why am I still alive?"

"Because I didn't want to kill you," Nefele replied. Her alarming honesty was followed by a gush of relief, filling her body with warmth. "Why did you come to find me?"

"Because I want it all to be over," he said, repeating again her earlier thoughts. This was her magic, Nefele realised. It hadn't changed his body but it had awoken the same desire in him, forcing him to act where she failed. "I can't live like this anymore. Like an animal. Even they have some level of companionship. I want it all to end."

She contemplated his words, wondering if the desire had manifested in the same way she meant it. "Do you want to die?"

"No!" he protested. "But death is better than this!" he said and pointed towards the window, to the outside. Nefele turned her eyes towards the see-through glass and smiled.

"I wanted it all to be over too," she admitted, the dangerous honesty slipping through her lips for a second time. "But in order to reclaim the outside. While I knew you walked over the island, I felt under constant threat and scrutiny, expecting you to attack me any time I ventured in the forest." She laughed and crossed her arms.

* * *

Nefele was often puzzled by how different magic had translated her desires. It could have taken many forms to manifest her wish but it chose the most complicated one. And the most cathartic. She had to move beyond the knowledge of the red book to find her answers on the nature of magic.

* * *

Simon didn't join her but appeared to relax the more she laughed. "I did as you asked and stayed away."

"I know," Nefele said. "Where were you? Where did you sleep all this time?"

"I built a small hut. Nothing special. I used mostly dead wood, just to give me some shelter at night."

"Where?" she asked him.

"I am not sure how to give directions for this place. What is north and what is south?"

"What was around the place you built your hut?"

Simon shrugged. Nefele's smile fell but she forced her lips to stretch again, afraid that her disappointment would destroy the new-found ease between them. She recognised it for an illusion, and a part of her preferred it for that. It was fictional, but it was also simpler, like the fairy tales that had given shape to her island life. "You can maybe show me?" she suggested.

He nodded. There was another pause between them until Simon found the courage to look at her again. "So you are not going to kill me?"

Her previous alarming honesty clashed with her survival instinct, the story of Abigail and Eleanor ringing in her mind. Nefele's eyes travelled to the stained-glass panels, a series of lonely women. What she had once viewed as supreme strength in her childish mind, as honour that touched divinity, whether that originated from the god of her parents or older ones was irrelevant, had lost all its glamour. It reeked of despair and injustice. All the stories she had read, all the diaries told the same tale. These were women who had either been forced to stay on the island to die or had fled the world because it was cruel and unjust to them. But Nefele was neither story.

"No," she whispered. Her eyes stayed on the panels. "What do you think of them?" she asked him.

Simon turned around and studied the glass. "They are beautiful."

Nefele hummed in agreement. "But what do they make you think? Why do you think they were made?"

He glanced at her, and in the corner of her eyes she saw another look of suspicion. It didn't last long and Simon studied the windows again. "They remind me of church," he finally said. "I hated church growing up—and still did when I turned into a man. But both my mother and my wife insisted we go every week. Our church had windows like that, filled with angels. I always thought they made them to keep men like me inside. To give us something interesting enough to focus on until we could escape the sermons."

"So you think they are shackles. Or traps."

There was another silence, more tiring than the first two. This one was broken by Simon. "Who are they?"

Nefele smiled sadly at him. "They are me," she said. "My past and future."

Simon looked between her and the panels a couple of

times. Nefele watched thoughts form and reform behind his eyes: suspicions, assumptions, and memories of old stories fighting against each other as he tried to decipher her truth. She waited for him to find it, not willing to expose herself but partly eager for him to succeed. The island had taught her that none of its joys could be gained without effort, and however unorthodox or temporary Simon's stay was on the island, for the time being he was one of its residents.

"Do you want to bathe?" she asked him. "We don't have warm water but there is a clear lake you can use. I can ask my elks to take you."

Simon's eyes widened at their mention. He shook his head profusely. "I don't like them. They scare me."

Nefele frowned. "They are lovely," she said, defending them.

"They are massive and make scary sounds. Their screams turned my dreams into nightmares."

She didn't pressure him. "I will go then," she said. He copied her as she stood up. She pointed at the boxes. "There should be clothes for a man somewhere."

"You really won't kill me?"

Nefele nodded. "I don't want to."

"Why?" Simon asked.

She shrugged. "Does it matter?"

Sounds from upstairs were heard. Nefele smiled as Auntie stumbled around until they made their way to the bottom floor. They took Nefele's outstretched hand. "Do not follow us," Nefele warned him. "I will do the same when you wish to bathe or change clothes."

He blushed at her words. Something in her chest

swelled with pride at his reddened cheeks but she didn't pay it much notice. She guided Auntie to the antechamber cave. While they waited for her elks to arrive so they could travel to the lake, Nefele stared at the closed door. For a few seconds she panicked that when she returned, it would be locked and Simon would have declared war on her for the island. Then, her worries calmed because it didn't matter what he did. They had reached the boiling point and, eventually, it would all be over, one way or another.

CHAPTER EIGHT

When she returned to the treehouse, Nefele found Simon cleaning. She lingered by the door while he was on his knees, wiping the floors with a cloth. Auntie tried to walk forward but Nefele held them in place when she noticed their dirty shoes. She squatted down and removed them before taking her own off. The moment she let go of Auntie, they dashed away. Simon paused his movements when they approached him and only continued what he was doing after they had climbed up the ladder, hiding again from his view.

Nefele stepped carefully over the floor, trying to minimise the stains she left over it, until she reached the kitchen part of the floor. She reignited the fire, failing to hide her smile when she heard Simon gasp at the simplest form of the magic she wielded, and waited for the soup to begin bubbling. Too hungry after her swimming, Nefele tore a piece of the potato bread to eat before jumping upwards to sit on the kitchen counter and continue watching Simon clean.

He was smaller than when he had first come onto the island. Her overwhelming emotions had stopped her from noticing it before but he had lost a fair amount of mass while he stayed away from her. Still, the memory of a hard worker's body haunted his form. She recalled their conversation from months prior, of his wife and dead child, of his need to distance himself from that reality, and she felt an even greater feeling of shame. "You don't need to do that."

He stopped and straightened his back. One of his hands quickly moved to the lower part and began massaging it. "It's filthy."

"I know," she agreed. "But you can't waste your whole time cleaning it. I just do the parts I use."

Simon turned to her. "You use the whole floor. Don't you walk on it?"

Nefele shrugged. "You still don't need to do that."

He shifted his position until he was sitting with his legs crossed and looking towards her. "And what am I to do?"

She bit her bread, chewing while she contemplated. What could she offer him to do? "What do you know to do? What are your skills?"

"I can clean. I can repair things. I can hunt. I can fish. Whatever you need, I will find out how to do it."

"Can you read?" she asked.

Simon's eyes narrowed at her question and nodded. "But what value is reading here?"

Nefele laughed, before pointing upwards. "Did you not notice that there are floors full of books in this house? What is their purpose if not to be read?" He blushed at her words, this time not out of shyness but embarrassment.

"Life on the island is hard, and harsh. It is no place for

softness and all its joys are hard earned. We cannot hunt the few animals *on* the island. They are our friends and cohabitants but we can fish. There is a cellar below with food supplies. You know about my vegetable garden as well. If an animal dies and we get to it fast enough, we can eat it too." She listed the main rules of the island, all she had learned with difficulty but offered to him as simple words.

* * *

This was unwise. It didn't reinforce the lesson that nothing came easy to those who inhabited the island. It did not matter that Nefele's confidant proved to be trustworthy and obedient. Every person who wishes to be the witch MUST work hard to understand the island.

* * *

"Let's go fish then," Simon suggested later that day. "Do you have a boat to move beyond the shore?"

Nefele shook her head. "I can't leave the island," she explained, another rule set by the diaries and the lore around the Floating Forest. He nodded, letting the information sink in, before standing up and offering her his hand. "Let's see what we can catch from the rocky beach then. Do you have a net, or a rod?"

"Both."

While they travelled to the stony shore, the gang leader of the elk herd appeared but didn't approach then. Simon stepped behind Nefele, who waved at the animal. They stared at each other, whispering through their eyes questions, objections, and warnings. Nefele understood them all but she pleaded with the elk to allow her to do as she pleased until the animal bowed his head and turned away.

"Let's continue," she suggested to Simon once the elk's footsteps had ceased.

When they reached the shore, Nefele allowed Simon to take charge as he set the net and sat next to him over the edge of the rock. Both of their feet dangled above the water, with waves occasionally rising high enough to wet their toes. Simon's eyes stayed fixed on the net, removing whatever they caught and putting it in the bucket they carried with them. Despite the wind having a soft bite and the smell of fish and sea being especially strong, the sun shone in between the clouds and Nefele lay backwards over the rock and basked under it. The initial discomfort of the prickling sensation underneath her eased and she nearly drifted to sleep, barely registering the whispered caress over her arm as Simon lay down too.

The direct sunlight had diminished her sight, filling it with spots of colours as she opened her eyes and turned her head to look at Simon. In the romance books she had read, these moments lead to romantic scenes, adding an additional layer to the sexual acts that anatomy books described. In the diaries, many of the previous witches alluded to such relationships before their time on the island. They took various forms, and their past lovers were sometimes remembered with nostalgia while others cursed them.

"What was your wife like?" she asked him.

Nefele watched her own reflection in his eyes, fascinated by their every movement and all the details she could pick out when their faces were so close. "I don't want to think about her."

"I understand."

"Have you ever had a husband?"

If she decided to respond as the witch, she had many lovers, in that ancient world her story originated from. If she was all the women who had been the witch, holding up the myth, then she had had even more lovers and husbands. She was maiden, mother, and crone, in a liminal space outside of time.

"No." She decided to simply be Nefele.

"Where I am from, they said that you were banished in this island by your former daughter-in-law, after you tried to seduce her fiancé and future king. That you wanted to tempt him into your bed, enchanting him with love potions and vile magic, so you could become queen again."

It was a tale she hadn't heard about the Floating Forest, even though some details sounded familiar. "I have never had a daughter-in-law," she replied and turned her head back to the sky, closing her eyes again.

"Is most of it a lie? The myth and the evilness?"

Before she had the chance to answer, a larger wave rose and crashed against them. Simon let out a yelp before he turned to secure their bucket but Nefele continued lying on the rock. The lulling warmth faded and soon her skin hair prickled as a shivering sensation overcame her. The wind's bite became harder and she brought her hands over her chest, rubbing her arms to reduce the cold.

She stopped when the sun peaked through the clouds again. The sea's rhythmic movement nearly quietened her to sleep, if not for the cold snaps against her toes and the voice in her mind that warned not to lower her defences completely. Simon didn't lie back down with her again, neither did they speak again while he fished.

"I think we have enough," he declared when the sun disappeared again. Nefele opened her eyes and faced a much darker sky, filled with deep grey clouds.

"It's going to rain." She took her feet out of the sea and stood up. Her trousers had mostly dried and she rolled her cuffs down. "We should hurry back. It is a harsh pour usually."

* * *

By the time they reached the treehouse, the rain had begun. Large, thick drops of water splashed around them, breaking through most of the protection that the trees and plants afforded them. Simon had wrapped the net over the bucket to protect their food but they were soaked to the bone by the time they reached the cave where the front door was.

Auntie was sitting on the yellow sofa, waiting for them.

They splattered water, drenching the floors that Simon had cleaned, as Nefele guided them to the kitchen. The bucket was disposed over the table as Nefele placed her hands over a fresh log and gave birth to a new flame. A small gulp escaped her lips as her desire for warmth nearly brought blistering heat over her skin. Unlike the first time that he had seen her exercise her magic, Simon showed signs of neither surprise nor fear. He squatted by the fire, eager to be warm and dry. Both of their shirts were stuck over their skins, hinting at the bodies underneath, and Nefele scolded herself for even thinking like that. The burning wood came with small puffs of smoke that made her eyes itch but she was too cold to rub them away. She focused on the sound of the cackling wood as hers and Simon's breaths evened out.

Auntie walked behind them and placed a woolly blanket over their shoulders. Both of their hands grabbed their respective edges, bringing their bodies closer, eager for more warmth. Auntie caressed with one hand each of their heads before they awkwardly sat on a chair.

"Thank you," Simon muttered, looking at them. "Auntie."

* * *

After they dried, Nefele picked a new set of clothes and went to the first floor to change while Simon searched through the box for any garments that could fit him. She waited by the ladder until he called her to come down, honouring the deal they had made to respect each other's privacy. He wore a long dark shirt over a pair of trousers that were too small for him while his clothes were hanging over one of the kitchen chairs. She did the same with her clothes as he took one of the fish out of the bucket.

"Do you have a sharp knife so I can gut and clean it?"

She pointed to a kitchen drawer. He picked one up and inspected it. "It needs sharpening. Where are your tools?" Nefele pointed to one of the lower cupboards. She pulled her body upwards to sit on the kitchen counter as Simon sharpened the knife.

"You don't need to do that," she said.

"I can cook," Simon said. His tone was flat and his simple words allowed for no protest, and Nefele had no real reason to. She hated cleaning fish and, after she had offered to relieve him of that duty, there was no reason to feel that he was being used. "If you want to do anything else, you can. You don't need to keep me company."

All her work on translation had ceased ever since she thought she had killed him. Nefele looked at the ladder as her desire for personal space battled against her fear of how he could claim the house while she left him alone. And yet, she had decided she wouldn't kill him, thus she had little option but to trust him, to welcome him into the treehouse.

"I will read then," she said and jumped down. She climbed to her desk and examined the diary with her notes scribbled in a blank paper next to it. She couldn't read them in front of Simon, not yet at least. It was one of the island's best kept secrets, ones Nefele had taken years to uncover, and held within them the path to conquering the island. The black cat that came and went as she pleased was sleeping on the armchair Auntie usually sat on.

* * *

The cat died in that armchair a few days later. The feline never forgave Nefele for replacing its previous owner, thus their cohabitation never turned to true friendship. She made sporadic appearances, mostly to hide from bad rain, hissing and scratching Nefele, showing favouritism to Auntie, and remaining a loyal familiar to the previous witch.

* * *

She picked up the romance novel she had last started and returned to the lower ground, sat in the kitchen area where Simon was still sharpening the knife.

A loud bang was heard and Simon looked up. "Auntie," Nefele explained. "They struggle amid the bookcases." When she caught his inquisitive eyes, she added, "They will be fine. They are coming down soon."

He parted his lips but said nothing. When he resumed working on the knife, Nefele turned her attention to her book. She flipped through it until she saw a part she recognised and started reading, but unlike other times, her mind failed to travel through the pages. Instead, every so often, she lowered the book to steal a look at Simon as he cooked.

"What books does the house have?" Simon asked, breaking the silence.

"Various. Stories, historical accounts, poems. Treatises on plants, on history." In her mind there was no subject that her library didn't have information about but ever since Nefele had begun reading, she had solely focused on her very narrow interests. It was likely that her library held many gaps and was mostly focused on information about the island. "I can find you something if you want? What are your interests?"

"I'll think about it," Simon said.

The idea of him browsing through the books, of going to her desk and finding the diaries and all their secrets, terrified her. She could accompany him all day, navigating him away from these texts, but it would only be a temporary measure, until he left or she told him the truth. Either way, Nefele was resolved to not kill him. Or anyone else. The pain of her dreams, the weight of the guilt. She couldn't have that again—never again.

She hid behind her book, moving pages without reading so she could maintain her lie of not being affected by him while Simon prepared their food. Every so often he would pause and ask her a question when he needed a new kind of utensil or tool, until, eventually, he placed all of their catch into spits and let them roast by the fire. He sat on the table, pulling at the too-tight trousers to get comfortable. Nefele lowered her book and found him studying her.

"What is your plan?"

"What plan?"

"Your plan with me. What are you going to do with me?"

She closed her booked and mimicked his pose, folding her arms over her chest. "I told you that I don't want to kill you."

He huffed. "That's not a plan, though. What do you want to do with me during the day, during the night? What am I supposed to be?"

It was all the questions Nefele had searched the diaries to find an answer to. Any other answer but that he was to be either her prey or her hunter. That their lives could coexist without murder. "You can do and be whatever you want," she said. "I can't decide your fate." Because if she did, then how would he be any different than Auntie? If she chose his role and his status, his place in the world, wouldn't she have stripped him of all identity as well?

Auntie jumped down the last few steps of the ladder. Both Nefele and Simon turned to look at them as they stood still, until they decided to walk to the couch, where they sat, instead of joining them in the kitchen. "Is this the plan? To turn me like Auntie?"

"No." Nefele shook her head. "I will never do that again."

"Then what is the plan for me?"

Nefele opened her book and hid behind the pages. Her eyes fixated on the letters but she remained unable to read them. "Whatever you want, that's the plan. Your future, your fate, that's for you to decide."

"What if I can't?" he mumbled.

"Then you should read a book," Nefele said. "That's what I did."

The smell of cooked fish began taking over the room and there was a loud cackling of the fire as one of the logs broke in two, sounding like a hag's screech of surprise. Neither of them said anything more for the rest of the evening. The rain against the glasses eased long after they ate and the bottom floor was only lit by the dying flame of the kitchen stove.

Simon's smoke-roasted fish were tastier than anything Nefele had ever cooked. Without needing to be asked, he broke the crab shells and placed them on her plate, allowing her to eat easily. The act was simple and required little effort but Nefele's heart clenched when she took the cracked crustacean and sucked on its tasty juices. It was also familiar, born from old memories of a good brother and an attentive father, foggy in her mind but also distinguishable as soft and kind. Nefele oscillated between her desire to lean into that kindness, that human companionship, and her rule that she was no longer anyone's sister or daughter.

"My only plan is to avoid killing you."

Simon cracked another crab and brought it to his mouth, pressing his lips over the dark red shell and slurping the tasty juices before snapping the crab shell in half and removing the white flesh with his fingers. "It's tasty," he said. Nefele nodded, happy for the change of subject and the extension they were both given to deciding their future.

CHAPTER NINE

They piled the dirty dishes upon their earlier ones, securing them enough to ensure there would be no broken glasses the next morning. Nefele added two fresh logs in the fire for the night and turned to Simon. "Take the bed," she suggested.

"It's your bed," Simon said. "I have already slept in it once."

"I can keep myself warm more easily," Nefele countered. "You might need a second blanket, though," she muttered and dashed to her pile of boxes. "This one is damp. I am sure I have more somewhere."

"I am not taking your bed," Simon said. "I can sleep by the fire."

Nefele lifted a box down and opened it. "You are not a dog," she replied, words both alien and familiar. Did her family own a dog? Were these her mother's words from once upon a time ago? "You are my guest."

"I will be fine on the couch."

"I insist you take the bed," Nefele said. "I want you to take the bed."

"What kind of man would I be if I took a lady's bed?"

Her cheeks flushed and an involuntary smile spread over her lips. "I am not a lady," she said but failed to hide the mirth from her tone. "I am the evil witch that gave you nightmares at night."

She found a dry blanket and handed it to him. He took it without any further arguments and Nefele smiled at her apparent victory while she continued shuffling through the fabrics until she found another blanket. Simon remained still, holding the blanket in his embrace, studying her. "I was never afraid of you," he said. "You have never given me any nightmares."

"I did leave you to starve in the wild, though."

* * *

The basis of all myths relies on the lack of details and the fluidity of time and space. The more concrete any of their stories become, the easier it is for both children and adults to dismantle them. The Floating Forest is no exception. In that regard, Nefele was a terrible witch impersonator. Her identity relentlessly interrupted her witch persona.

* * *

Their arguments about the bed continued for days, with Nefele's insistence that she surrender her comfort to Simon winning every night. Their lives settled into a predictable rhythm, dominated primarily by the daily upkeep of the house and their survival needs. Unlike the union of Eleanor and Abigail, Nefele didn't abdicate her responsibilities towards the house or the island. She dirtied her hands gardening, wet her bare feet into the sea, and sweated, but the additional pair of hands made a significant difference, allowing more free time for both of them.

"I am not taking the bed tonight," Simon said, starting anew their nightly argument. "It's your turn."

"No," Nefele said. "You need it more than I do."

"I am rested now. You can have it back."

"But the couch is too small for you, Simon," Nefele said. She had got into the habit of adding his name at the end of most of her sentences. "Auntie keeps me company."

"I am sleeping down here tonight. Either you take the bed, or it stays empty." Simon folded his arms, tapping his foot on the ground.

"Simon," Nefele scolded him. Without another word, he dashed to the couch and lay on it, keeping his arms folded over his chest and his longer legs curled slightly at the knees because the furniture was too small for him. "You will be sore tomorrow," she pointed out.

"You are sore too. I have noticed your groaning."

It was the truth. Although Nefele could fit better than him, sleeping at the odd angle had taken its toll on her body. The velvet material overheated her and some springs were poking her in painful spots that remained perma-nently sore throughout the day. She did want her bed back.

"It is not productive for one of us to suffer though," Nefele muttered. "None of us can survive without proper rest. Life here is very physical and we need all the strength we can muster from our sleep."

"I am glad you agree. Go to bed now."

"Come with me," Nefele suggested, the reckless words spilling out of her mouth before she could think them over, or digest how they sounded. Her face burned while her mind conjured images from her books, of potential love interests who were forced to share a bed and how this led to their bodily desires being exposed. Simon made a choking sound and sat up on the couch, looking at her with guarded hesitation. It took Nefele a few moments to conclude that he hadn't rejected her outright. He had a wife, and a dead child. Simon knew the secondary meaning masquerading behind her words.

He had a wife. Simon had a wife.

"I don't wish for that," Nefele clarified as the silence between them continued. "We can put a pillow between us, if you are afraid of me."

That same look of suspicion battling with confusion passed over his face. "There is no need for a pillow," Simon said. "None of us are virgins after all."

Nefele forced her facial muscles to remain loose before she turned around and climbed the ladder. His eyes burned her neck and back as he followed her, looking at her, and she couldn't stop herself from thinking that he was imagining her in bed with him, like in the novels, experienced and seductive, knowledgeable about all the ways men could be pleasured because she was ancient and knew more about everything than anyone else.

Or it was bait.

Auntie followed after them but stopped on the third floor, turning towards the narrow spaces between the bookcases instead of following them to the fourth level where the bed was. The only bed, because there was no need for any more beds. Because the witch lived alone and, if a man stumbled upon the island, she wasn't a virginal little girl who only knew of lovemaking from books.

It was bait. Simon was uncovering more and more of the truth with each passing day.

"I am going to change into a nightdress," she told him before he climbed the final ladder. He nodded and stayed downstairs while Nefele discarded her dress and put on a white, thin nightgown. She waved at him to come and was in bed before he had climbed upstairs.

"I sleep without the trousers, just in a plain shirt," he said. She turned her head away from him while he took off his clothes, pulling the covers close to her face to avoid looking at him. He put on a loose shirt, one of the many male clothes he seemed to be finding on the island ever since their cohabitation had started. The bed dipped when he went under the covers and his body warmth filled Nefele with tension while she failed to stop herself from inhaling deeply his natural smell. She clasped her hands together and pressed them against her chest, while she focused on the nightly sounds of the island and his breathing.

Not long after he came to bed, Simon shifted to lie on his back and his foot touched hers. Nefele spasmed slightly at the touch. "Goodnight, Witch," he whispered.

"Goodnight," Nefele replied.

Sleep didn't come for Nefele and she feared that Simon was lying awake next to her, waiting like a hawk to catch her when she changed positions. She pressed her eyes shut and began counting, an exercise she hadn't needed to do for years because sleep always came easy before. Before Simon had arrived, when work was hard, her body ached for rest and the whole island was safe.

Why? Why? Why had she said what she did? It would have been better if they both slept on the bottom floor, or if they used the bed on alternate days each. There were so many better options than their current predicament.

"Are you sure you don't need the pillow between us?" he asked.

Bait.

Nefele kept quiet, counting with religious fervour until, after what felt like hours, Simon's breathing changed and he turned to his side, offering her his back.

* * *

Nefele claimed that offering her bed held no secret motives. She insisted upon that for years to come, blaming the romance novels for her flushes and wild imagination. She blamed her youthful body, and its natural tendencies, all necessary for procreation if she wasn't the witch of the Floating Forest but a simple girl, meant to get married and become a mother. In truth, loneliness was the root of her decision. She wished to be touched. Not the empty caresses of Auntie, devoid of reciprocal affection and simply a magical reflection of her needs, but the feeling of another on her body. It wasn't sexual desire, this came later, but the need to be held, to feel fully and unapologetically the presence of someone else.

Don't blame her.

* * *

They woke up in each other's embrace, nearly at the same time. Their legs were tangled and they held each other's clothes, while their faces had drifted close enough to feel each other's breath. Simon moved first, adding distance between them without getting up. Nefele sat up, pulling the covers towards her chest, her mind empty for a moment.

The previous day's cloudy weather had subsided and the room was lit completely by the direct sunlight, making the smell of their sleep and sweat more prominent. "We need to air the room," Nefele said, focusing on the practical —and inconsequential—element over the complicated embarrassment she felt over their earlier position. And the memory of his skin against hers, the way she missed holding onto his shirt. How uncomfortably empty her fist was. Or how her skin protested returning to her usual solitary existence.

Simon appeared hurt—and offended—by her words, but Nefele attributed the look to her own confused state, rather than a true reflection of his feelings.

"I will change downstairs and start breakfast," she said and fled.

She had finished setting up the table when Simon appeared again, followed by Auntie. He steadied their body, helping them land safely on the floor. His wariness of them had vanished and his attitude towards them had changed to that of an older brother—or even father—as he helped them in their daily life. Nefele was grateful that he never asked for Auntie's story, even though if Simon stayed with her, the topic would eventually arise.

He sat at his usual chair and she took her place opposite

of him. It terrified her how easily they had set to having their own places in the house, or how they had divided tasks and both knew who was carrying what when they went outside. The easiness was sweet like honey and it tangled all over Nefele's body, bringing up images of dead flies caught in a trap jar, lured by the smell of deliciousness. By the time they realised it was a trap, their bodies were not their own anymore and their death imminent.

But the sweetness was comforting and while Nefele's logic rang all her inner alarm bells that she ought to tread carefully, she failed to listen to them. "I will go fish again," Simon said. "Now that the sun is up and should remain dry throughout the day, we can have something other than vegetables."

"We can make crab soup," Nefele suggested.

"I don't want soup. I want to cook them by the fire again."

She nodded. "I'll come with you."

He smiled. "Maybe we can both bring a book, and read by the sea," he suggested. "Would you recommend me one?"

* * *

The days turned into weeks and the weeks into four months since they had begun living together. They never strayed far from each other but Nefele had eased her rules of keeping Simon always by her side, except from wandering in the library. It was fortunate that Simon didn't desire to read a lot, content to be given books and trusting of Nefele's knowledge when he asked for reading material on a specific topic. Like her own younger self, he gravitated towards the story books, filled with pictures, but he was growing hungrier day by day for myths about the Floating Forest. Often, he would ask her questions, laced with curiosity, about her own story, fact checking the myths against her reality. Nefele played along and made up a new version of herself, an amalgamation of the women whose diaries she had read.

His eyes shone with suspicion more often than confusion but whenever he caught her in a lie, Simon never pressed for a confession, playing along himself at the façade that he was a witch's companion. They held onto each other during their sleep without ever discussing again the concept of past lovers and what their bedsharing made them.

The only thorn of their cohabitation was that Nefele hadn't found a way to read more journals without being found during the day. Or rather, she still didn't feel safe enough to risk leaving Simon alone long enough to go to her desk and continue her translating. One fear led to another and crippled all her desires to progress in her research of finding a story—any kind of sign—that what she was doing with Simon was allowed.

* * *

~~I think~~ Perhaps it was fear that crippled her the most. What would she do if she read all the diaries and there was no precedent to what she desperately wanted?

* * *

Her only option was to read at night, sacrificing her rest for the pleasures of knowledge and satisfying her growing curiosity. It took her three weeks to study Simon's sleeping habits, to test how easily he woke when she got out of bed or whether a small noise would wake him. The first night she dared her escapade, Nefele's stomach was tangled in knots, phantom pains made her legs wobble, and more than once she considered retreating to bed.

She only relaxed when she climbed down the ladder and walked on the tips of her toes to reach her desk. Auntie, roused from their hiding place amid the books, made their way to Nefele, sitting at their old spot, while the young witch sat at her desk and lit an old candle.

"Like old times, Auntie," Nefele whispered. She put her finger over her lips, as if the other creature had a way of speaking, and smiled at them. "This will be our secret."

Auntie tilted their face and their faceless empty existence turned towards her. All the months—how long had it been?—that Auntie had lived with Nefele, she had avoided looking at their face, only allowing passing glances, but that night, she stared at them, her greatest magical achievement, the most powerful spell she had ever cast. Auntie's face betrayed a bone structure beneath it, even though it was minimal. There were bumps indicating where their cheeks were, and small hollows where their eye-sockets should be. They looked like the early stages of a sculpture, having a general shape but missing all the identifying features to transform them into a work of art. All their half-shaped, smudged-over characteristics reminded Nefele of the mother they once were. She haunted Auntie's face, never allowing the world to forget that she had once occupied that body.

"I am sorry," she whispered to them. "I am very sorry." She wiped her eyes, even though she didn't shed any for Auntie. The act was performative, allowing Nefele to end the emotional sidetrack her mind had taken her, before she turned to her papers.

She scribbled words, searching the dictionary for them and trying to make sense as she moved them about the page, until they formed any coherent meaning.

* * *

It was sloppy, unmethodical work. Nefele got better as the years passed but her work required the touch of a proper linguist. ~~I am sure the island will find a better linguist witch than me one day.~~ The Floating Forest will eventually attract such a person to improve Nefele's work.

* * *

Nefele yawned as she browsed the collection, searching for a book on elks for Simon. His relationship with them had remained tense, although he no longer hid behind her whenever they appeared, but he wished to know more about the species so he could vanquish his fears and approach them like Nefele and Auntie did. There were many books on the subject, some written in old languages that neither of them spoke, others filled with images but few words. Her fingers trailed the spines as she read them, lifting off a light wave of dust until she stopped in front of a small book, a bit bigger than her palm, titled *The Mythology of Elks*. She pulled the book out, only to see a stack of papers stashed behind it. Nefele reached for them. She secured the book under her armpit and studied the papers, written in her native tongue. The first page wasn't the correct first one as it began mid-sentence but it was clearly a diary—or rather a part of it—that she had found.

She went quickly to her desk, hiding the papers in a drawer before returning to the ground floor where Simon waited for her. "Here you go." She handed him the book.

"The Mythology of Elks," he read the title. "Are you sure this won't frighten me further?"

Nefele shook her head, even though she had no knowledge of the book's content. "It will help you understand that, like any animal, the elks have their mythos, but because we humans conjure stories about them, that doesn't make them real. It's only our imagination being placed upon something unknown to us."

"Hm," he mumbled but accepted the book. "I was thinking we could go to the north part of the island." He pointed towards the back of the house, where he claimed the north was. "I have never seen it."

Her tongue twisted in her mouth and her throat clenched as if she was suffocating. That section of the island was where the beach her father's boat had landed and then disappeared. And where she had pushed Auntie's children back into the water, sending them to their death.

She nodded. If she refused to traverse there, Simon would need an explanation. Nefele could lie, claim there were monsters or dangerous magic, but her tongue refused to speak the excuse. She feared her words would tremble as they came out of her mouth, reeking of lies to the point that Simon would have no choice but to ask her for more information. She followed after him with her head lowered and offering short answers to Simon's continuous attempts to instigate a conversation.

"Look at that!" he said, grabbing her hand. Nefele nearly lost her balance as he pulled her towards a sunken built square. There were four small pillars, rising no higher than the ground, and the floor was a mixture of stones and wildflowers. "What is this place?"

Nefele had read about it, and vaguely remembered seeing it during her early exploration days, when she was less focused on the past and her regrets. "It's a sunken garden," she said.

"How do you get down there? There are no stairs to get back up."

"You are not supposed to get back up," Nefele whispered and her hand stretched towards Simon. The thought of pushing him and letting the wild nature of the island have its way with him entered her thought with frightening ease. Her finger touched his shirt and grabbed it in her fist, pulling him away from the edge. "It's a death sentence," she said. "There are deadly insects living in it."

Simon's eyes narrowed but he heeded her warning and moved a step back. They stared at the hole. "The pillars. Why?"

Nefele remembered reading about them. "So the victim can climb up to evade the insects, until they succumb to the poison and fall back down, to be consumed."

Simon stretched his neck to look at the bottom of the hole. "There are no bones though."

She shrugged, not knowing the answer and only able to imagine horrible reasons for the skeletons' absences. When she stole a glance towards Simon, he was studying her, not with the usual look of suspicion or even confusion, but fearfully, like she was a monster. Nefele smiled at him but didn't offer any further words. She wanted him to stop looking at her like that, to bring the glint of amusement in his eyes and banish the blank fear that blinded him. Breathing was difficult and the world threatened to start spinning if she didn't calm down but she was trapped in his empty gaze, unable to escape it without him leaving it too.

He broke their eye contact for a second glance at the garden, before he sighed and offered her his hand, without looking at her. "Let's go."

Nefele grabbed it, holding it tightly as her fingers moved between his and she squeezed with all her might. It didn't occur to her this was another first between them, or that it shifted their relationship further onto dangerous paths. Nefele only welcomed the comfort of his touch and the extension he offered for them to continue living as they did.

* * *

Nefele was right to fear that moment. Her old spell asking for it "all to end" was still active and the end hadn't been decided yet.

* * *

They settled on a sandy beach, although Nefele was certain it wasn't the one where she had first landed, filled with large rocks blocking the horizon view. Simon set the net for his catch while Nefele lay a sheet on the sand for them. She placed both of their books on it and sat with her back against one of the rocks. When Simon returned, he surprised her by sitting right next to her, with their arms and thighs touching each other. He didn't pick up the book she had chosen for him but instead he snaked his hand to find hers and held it. He gazed at the shore, where the water met the sand, and after a few moments, Nefele relaxed and leaned towards him, allowing her head to rest against his shoulder.

She didn't know how long they were like that but when Simon turned and kissed her temple, her other hand jumped upwards and grabbed his arm. Her nails dug into his skin and she pressed her face against his shirt-covered body, inhaling him. Simon shifted and enveloped her in a hug. The details faded until Nefele was on her back against the sun-warmed sheet, with Simon lying partly on top of her and his tongue trying to separate her lips.

She was afraid of giving in but another, deeper kind of fear took over because she didn't want to lose him. Her hands grabbed his waist and pulled him closer to her as she parted her lips and they kissed. An instinctual drive possessed her, moving her body and forming sounds she had never made before while her ears drunk all the noises that escaped Simon.

They stopped only when both of their eyes opened. Nefele lay back her head while Simon was still propped up above her, breathing hard. "How many faces can you put on?" he asked as his thumb played with her bottom lip. He lowered his body and kissed her again before he released her to lie next to her, like they did in bed. Then he started laughing.

Her excitement faded as his laughing intensified and she wanted him to stop. She moved away from him but before she was able to get up, he grabbed her hand and pulled her towards him. "Kiss me again," he asked.

Was it another truce extension or bait? Nefele feared every truce she formed with him was such a trap but she found her resolve weak. All her usual fears of losing the island, or even her life, paled in comparison to facing him against her—and returning to her earlier life devoid of human contact. She lifted her body until she found his lips again, certain that there was relief in Simon's eyes thanks to her choice.

CHAPTER TEN

Nefele ignored the new diary she had found that night, preferring to rest holding onto Simon instead of searching for the truth of the island and whether what she was doing with him had any kind of precedence. It wouldn't matter, she decided, because she wanted to keep him, and continue whatever they had.

In the morning, the warmth and elation of the previous day had faded. It was the first time in weeks that she had woken up before him. She put on a dress and left the bedroom, afraid of his reaction to all they had done the previous day—What if it was regret? What if he pretended that nothing had happened? What if he blamed her?—and to disturbing his sleep.

She went to her desk, where Auntie was already sitting, as if they were waiting to scold Nefele for all the rules she had broken. They sat not in their usual armchair but on Nefele's chair behind the desk, with their arms folded against their shapeless chest. "Are you upset with me?"

Auntie didn't move. Nefele wasn't sure what she expected from them, but her skin prickled with discomfort when she noticed a blank piece of paper in front of them, which she couldn't remember leaving there. "I know what I am doing," she said, protesting Auntie's silence—as if she could expect anything but it from them.

She said more while she waited for Auntie to react in any way, stopping only when Nefele realised she was para-phrasing books and the excuses young women who were discovered to have strayed from the path of propriety said in defence of their actions. She only realised it because her last one was "he loves me", a clear lie. Her half-uttered sentence turned into a choke which then became a coughing fit. Her lungs contracted as if she was not only trying to clear a blockage but to spit the lies out of her system before they poisoned her completely. Her eyes filled with tears as she tried to regain her breath but they kept rolling down her face.

"I am sorry."

She ran down the stairs, feeling like the house would collapse around her and her lungs would collapse against her ribcage if she didn't have any fresh air. She stumbled her way down the stairs to the cave entrance where her elk, her dearest and oldest friend and ally, waited.

"I am sorry," she repeated and reached for the animal.

He stared down at her, like the demonic creature that Eleanor and Simon thought them to be, before he stepped forward and pressed his large nose against her palm. Her fingers curled against his fur but the elk didn't complain, nor tried to sever their contact. His breathing synchronised with Nefele's, until her own chest moved evenly and she managed to stand back up on her feet.

"Have I done something terrible?" she asked the animal. "Will you hate me from now on?"

The animal licked her face and Nefele hugged his head. She wished their love could contain language, clear words that could assuage all her guilt and offer guidance as to what she ought to do.

But she wanted to keep Simon. No matter what the diaries said or didn't say, she wanted to keep him. She wanted him to stay. Her desire to not kill him had evolved into that desperate need which defied all logic and clouded all thoughts. Whatever defences she had against that yearning were annihilated after their kissing and touching the previous day.

"Please don't make me choose you or him. Can't I just have him for me? Is it so terrible? The world doesn't need to know." The elk licked her again and gently pushed her towards the door with his head. "I will not kill him."

The elk rubbed his head against her, making his large antlers tap against one of the cave walls, and nudged her towards the door once again. "I love you. I am so grateful to you. If it wasn't for you, I would have died. Thank you for taking me in, for leading me here and standing guard while I grew up. But I—" She choked her next words. "I thought you should know, in case it all goes wrong."

Nefele wiped her newly gathered tears and went back inside. Auntie had followed her to the bottom floor, holding a stack of papers with both of their hands. She approached them and Auntie pressed the papers against her chest before they went to sit at the yellow couch. She watched them fold their arms and cross their legs. She hugged the papers against her chest and walked to the kitchen, sat at the table, and placed the papers on it.

Before reading them, she looked at the stained-glass women, each one trapped in their individual frame, being both majestic and pathetic in their solitude, as the sun pierced them and turned them into a further idealised version of their story. All that had remained of their identity was the fairy tale but this couldn't have been their only story. Rays of their colourful sunlight transformed the bottom floor of the tree house into a place of wonder while the see-through window of the kitchen area in contrast only emphasised the plainness of everyday life. She smelled the bread she and Simon had baked together and the remnants of the crabs they had roasted, even though he had taken the leftovers outside the previous night.

She flipped the pages so she could face the written words and began rearranging them in order to place them in the right chronology. Some were missing, and some seemed to be from different stories of the same person. The only ones that offered any kind of picture said:

never allowing him to stand too close. But my husband is determined to win them over. I think his effort is futile because my people think of elks as the protector of women, naturally hostile to men for that exact reason. They are the companions of girls, widows, and spinsters and find it hard when they bond with married women. But they are kind creatures, never being outrightly hostile to him for my sake.

Our time on the island has been peaceful and I have found magic to be an easy and dependable craft to learn, bettering our life at every opportunity and reflecting my desire for happiness. When we first sailed away, we could never have dreamed of such a home, but the Floating Forest— or the Traveling Haven as I grew up calling it—is the wish I never knew I cast upon the stars. My husband has only managed the barest of spells, complaining that the land doesn't respect his desires, but I fear it is because he does not wish to stay. He does not appreciate all this place offers us—a chance to be together away from prying eyes, scornful whispers, and constant threatening meddlers who cannot stand our union because it was sanctioned by two different gods.

He misses the company of other men, of other women even. I never feared he would be unfaithful, but I suspect he misses being wanted, admired as he once was. Here, his only role is to be my husband, and the only other dominant creatures tolerate him for their affection towards me—and, I hope, soon, the baby. He was pleased when I told him, I am sure. Rag always wanted to be a father. I only desire for this to have

There was no page to continue the sentence and the next instalment told of events months later.

He plans to leave but I can't. Not after what happened, what I did, all to keep us safe. Rag wishes to take our son, insisting that there cannot be a future for him here. What kind of lonely, empty life will he lead without any other humans but his mother and father? Or his mother only, because he cannot stay in a place that feeds its existence through terror and murder. It is not safe for our souls, he says.

It is as safe as we want to make it. I think.

We are at an impasse. My son cries for him every moment I have held him since that day. As if Latham knows that I have changed a bit too much. I am too witch to be his mother now. He cries so loudly the whole treehouse shakes and his body turns red from the wiggling to escape me. His revulsion for me is a dagger through my heart, a poisoned arrow that makes me wish there was a way to end my life so he could stop crying. He goes most of the day without milk until when he is exhausted and delirious from hunger he accepts my breast. Crying while he drinks.

Rag watches with saddened fury.

He says I must go with him, put this island behind us, and move on to the life we always ought to have. Vow to forget all the magic and never utter a word of two years here. He asks me to act as Lathan's mother, the only one he will ever have, and as his wife, the one he chose to have, but I cannot say the words because the witch doesn't leave the island. None of the diaries say such a thing.

And I cannot leave magic behind. I know that no matter how hard I try, there will come a day when our home will be in danger and my desire to survive and protect them will unleash a power the world has not seen since ancient times. I will have no control over it, and then I will doom all my people.

This is what he fails to understand. Men and women of my tribe have been called demons for whispers of magical practices, for a simple year of good luck. What will his people do if one of us actually turns the world into ruins?

They will try to eradicate the few of us that are left, including our son.

But he speaks of Latham's future and I know that there is none for my boy here. There are stories amid my people of the children raised in the wild and they all die lonely deaths.

At moments like this, I am ashamed to admit, I hate Latham. If it wasn't for him, I could have kept my husband. But it might take years until the next

Nefele flipped to the next page, which was not the direct continuation of the old witch's story.

Their sails were the same as the ones Rag and Latham followed. I have been counting the years since then. My son will be eleven, his boyhood will be over. In my imagination he is happy. I have tried to use magic to see him again, casting spells on the mirror, but my desire is not pure enough for there are only blurred colours that appear and muffled sounds enter my ears.

Or else what I am casting to see cannot be shown because they are no longer alive.

When I stood at the beach waiting to see if they would send me any boats filled with men, I naively hoped for Rag to be one of them. He was not. The men who came were of a different kind and they spoke the same threats, suggested they come to my bed and, because they were not reasonable, I put their corpses back into the boat.

I despise killing, although it has gotten easier, but I avoid it unless the visitors try to become intruders. They add to the stories of danger that mist over my island. My haven, which takes me all over the world but never brings me close enough to my native people's seaside residence, nor wherever my husband and child established their new home.

I still wish upon the stars at night but they never blink back at me anymore. I have spent my ratio of miracles. Now, I must continue the fairy tale.

The rest of the pages were fragments of other stories, mostly visits or reflections on the island's nature that Nefele didn't plan to investigate that morning. She brought her legs up onto the chair and hugged her knees as she stared at the words. She slowly rocked herself back and forth. Like the nameless witch, Nefele regretted the birth of that baby who had stolen her husband, leaving her alone on the island. She understood the witch's fears because she was mostly raised in the wilderness of the island.

"Hey," Simon said.

Nefele flipped the top page so there were no visible written words to him and turned to him.

"Were you crying?" he asked and moved towards her, cupping her face as his thumbs rubbed the top of her cheeks. "Is it about yesterday?"

She shook her head and placed her hands over his, pressing them further against her skin. "It is nothing."

He squatted so his eyes could be closer to her level and his hands held onto hers. "You can trust me," he said. "I don't know who or what kind of other men you have met, but you can trust me."

"Honey laced traps," her mind screamed, but Nefele couldn't help but smile. "It really is nothing," she tried to reassure him. Simon looked unconvinced but, like many times in the past, he pushed aside whatever concerns he had. He hugged her from the back, placing a soft kiss on her neck, making her shiver.

"What is that?" he inquired and extended his arm to pick up the loose pages on the table. Nefele slapped his hand away while she placed her other over the papers to stop him from taking them.

"A secret," she offered as an explanation.

Simon's initial dislike of her reaction faded as that usual

look of suspicion came over him. Auntie stood up and stumbled onto furniture, breaking some of the tension. They both turned towards them, waiting to see them getting back up and making their way to the ladder before they climbed upstairs.

"Is it a book? Are you writing a story?"

How much nicer would it be if all she had read in the diaries were people's fancies? She nodded, hoping this reduced Simon's interest in the pages, until she found the chance to hide them from him.

"Can I read it?"

"Not yet." After a moment's hesitation she lifted her hand that wasn't holding onto the papers and caressed him. His eyes moved downwards, looking down at her face.

"But one day?"

"One day." She was sincere.

"What is it about?"

She stretched her palm over the papers and caressed them with her fingertips. "My life."

* * *

They ended up back in bed before half the day had passed and most of their daily work was left unfinished, but Nefele couldn't resist her own hunger for his touches. They stumbled up the ladders, casting clothes floor to floor until they made it to the bed. She feared the whole house would fall down from the roughness of their movements and the creaking of her bed.

She used the edge of the sheet to clean her belly from his seed. She was grateful for the lesson from the papers.

Neither the island nor her body was a place for a baby. Simon didn't protest her decision when she asked him to pull out, neither did he look surprised that she was aware of conception. She was grateful her inexperience hadn't shown the previous day—or he had chosen to not question it— and there was no blood to betray that it was her first time. Simon breathed heavily next to her, his one hand playing with a strand of her hair while his other was placed over his slightly hairy chest. "I want to ask you something but I don't think now is the right time."

This was the beginning of their usual fact-checking game, where Nefele answered sometimes as the witch, sometimes as the castaway, and other times as the previous women, contradicting herself and allowing Simon openings of inquiry which he didn't take. She didn't doubt his intelligence, because she noticed his eyebrows furrowing when she said something that didn't match what he thought he knew about her. "Ask me. I might answer."

"You always answer," he said and kissed her shoulder. "Is Auntie older than you? Were they on the island when the gods trapped you here?"

All her bliss from the pleasure before slipped out of her and Nefele felt smaller inside her body. Like her insides had shrivelled and there was an invisible gap between her skin and her organs, filled only by emptiness. "I will tell you, if you answer my question."

Simon propped himself up. "What do you want to know?"

"About your wife. And your dead baby."

He tensed at her words and distanced himself from her. He had lost his own remaining bliss. A part of Nefele yearned to lean towards him, kiss him back into relaxation, and put the matter of questions and curiosity to rest. Another wanted to learn with a self-harming mania how she compared to that faceless woman and the beautiful baby that connected Simon to his wife. Her curiosity mingled with her desire to be punished, like in her dreams when she thought she had killed Simon, and her mind conjured scenarios of him imagining his wife while he slept with Nefele. It was a tense need that made her wish to find that woman, who was perfect, maidenly and motherly like a princess. The perfect antithesis to her role as the witch.

"Why do you want to know about them?" Simon asked.

"Because they are a part of you," she said, the words slipping out of her mouth unfiltered. "I hunger for all of you."

He appeared pleased with what she said and Nefele dreaded him telling her about them, because she would need to admit what she had done to Auntie and then he would see her as a monster. Then, it would all just end. Exactly like she wanted through her spell.

"Later." He moved closer to her, resuming his earlier position, and Nefele curled up to his chest, wrapping her arms around him. "Another day."

She kissed his sternum as her fingers played with the hair on it.

* * *

Anyone would think that Nefele was playing with fire. What she did was dangerous but it was not naivety nor lack of intel-

ligence that led her down that path. It was not even youthfulness and the influence of romance stories. What she desired was to confess and to untangle the witch from Nefele and Nefele from the rules of the diaries. This was the path she chose to walk, even if she did so unconsciously.

CHAPTER ELEVEN

Nefele waited for Simon's breathing to even before she got out of bed and tiptoed out of the bedroom. Leaving the bed had turned into a ritual that became easier every night she decided to act upon her curiosity to continue her work on translating the diaries. With practiced expertise she avoided every board that creaked, evaded every obstacle that might betray her, and climbed silently down.

Auntie waited at the desk, which they relinquished when Nefele appeared. "Thanks Auntie." Nefele pinched the candle with her thumb and her index finger, allowing a small flame to be born, fuelled by her desire to read. The soft orange glow of the flame illuminated the space and Nefele placed the candle into the metalling holder. She waited for the first few drops of wax to fall down, ensuring that it would stay in place, and then slipped into her chair. The smoke mixed with the smell of old paper and ink as she took her papers out of the secret compartment, alongside her notes on vocabulary, grammar, and the dictionary she used. Finally, she opened the notebook with her translations and picked up her work, mouthing the words in that other tongue as she tried to find their meaning.

"What are you doing up so late?" Simon asked.

Nefele startled at his voice. Her hand spasmed onto the paper, scratching a small hole through it. "Why are you up?"

"I noticed you weren't next to me, and I came looking for you." He approached her desk. Nefele glanced at Auntie, begging them silently to intervene, to offer a distraction as they so often did when Simon was too close to uncovering her secrets, but they remained seated, facing the wall with their legs crossed and their arms folded in their lap. "Why are you up?"

"I was working," Nefele said, hoping Simon was sleepy and would return to bed without asking for any further explanation until morning. She cursed inwardly when his eyes lost the last vestiges of sleep.

"Writing your book?" His eyes travelled to the opened dictionary.

Feeling caught, Nefele shook her head. "I am translating."

He walked behind her and she closed the notebook with her translated words and leaned back. "Is it another secret?"

"Yes."

She watched him scan the words of the original manuscript, his eyes moving side by side, as if he was reading them. Could he? She had no way of knowing because, despite their physical closeness and the companionship that had developed between them, Simon remained a stranger to Nefele. "Who wrote this?"

"I did," Nefele lied. "This is mine." Because she was the witch.

"Why are you translating it then?"

"For myself."

Simon leaned forward and picked the diary in the foreign tongue before Nefele could stop him.

"Give it back, Simon!"

He ran around the desk with Nefele chasing him but after three unsuccessful attempts, she gave up. This was the boiling point. This was the end she had wished for. Why evade it or attempt to prolong the lie? She turned to Auntie and extended her hand, waiting for them to come for comfort and support, but they remained still. Her hand hovered and the sting of their rejection hung in the air until she lowered it and she turned to Simon.

He reopened the notebook, and dragged his fingers over the foreign letters. "The pirates did not know the dangers of all they faced when they stared at my naked body," he translated. His voice trailed as he searched for the words, but it was clear that he was fluent in the language. "They ambushed me when I bathed. There were ten of them and only one of me but there was no reason to fear."

"Give it back to me, please," Nefele asked in a low voice. "Please, Simon. It's mine."

He closed the notebook and tossed it on the table. "Will you now hurt me? Will you finally show me the witch's evil face?"

The threats formed in her mouth, but Nefele found herself too tired to speak them. "No," she said. "I don't want to hurt you."

"What do you want then?"

Tears rolled down her face and she wiped them with the back of her hand. "Nothing," she lied because she wanted all of him. She wanted him to stay. She wanted it all to end. Her original desire to be left alone on the island again, to be free to dance and roam around the trees, had changed into wanting to walk it with him, to keep him but without lies and without the fear of the inevitable clash. "I have no right to want anything from you."

"Why?" Simon insisted. "What is so special about me that you treat me differently from all others?" He pointed to the notebook, where he had read of a witch who encountered ten pirates alone and lived to write her story.

Nefele let out a sob-turned-chuckle. "I simply do not want to, Simon." She moved to her desk and sat down again. "Go back to bed. I won't bother you. You should rest."

She sensed his hesitation to leave her and knew than when he did eventually turn around and leave her alone it wasn't the same as the other times that he had dropped a line of inquiry. This was the beginning of the end, her magical wish unfolding itself and pushing Simon—and Nefele—into achieving it.

* * *

When Nefele saw the sails of another ship the next morning, she couldn't help but smile, in surrender to her own magical will working its way to offering her the end she had originally wanted. It didn't matter that her desires had changed along with the context that surrounded the end she longed for. There was a strange sense of relief that washed over her when the ending of her story with Simon became clear. The loose diary pages, of a witch with a husband who abandoned her, were a foreshadow the house offered her, to prepare her for the reality that the truth wouldn't be tolerated and Simon would leave. And perhaps a push for her to enjoy the time she had with him, which Nefele doubted she would ever experience again.

She climbed to the top floor, where she found Simon sitting on the wooden boards and staring out through the south window, not the one that showed the vessel with the red sails. "A ship will be upon the island very soon," she said. She pointed to the west side window. "If they come close enough and send boats, would you like to follow them so you can return home?"

Simon stood up and walked past her to the window. His eyes were red with sleeplessness before he turned to Nefele with an expression of curled lips and watered eyes. He looked so young. Nefele often forgot that he was only a few years older than her. "Why?"

"Because you are a good man," she said. "And I set you free."

His face twitched and he wrapped his arms around himself as he doubled down and squatted to the floor again. His shoulders trembled as he cried and a few gasped sobs escaped him. "Why are you crying? Don't you want to go home? There is a whole world out there for you."

Simon's response was another gasp, which turned into a wail. Nefele's body froze with uncertainty and the crippling difficulty of deciding whether she ought to hug him and promise him that all would be well in the end or to leave him be, to afford him his privacy until he returned to his senses and left her. For a few long painful moments, they stayed fixed on their spots, but when Nefele found the strength to decide to turn around and descend the ladder, Simon grabbed her hand. "Why? Am I not good enough for you?"

His question broke all her resolve to remain aloof, to play the role of the witch and she shook her head emphatically. "No," she protested.

"Then why?!" His eyes widened with realisation. "Is it because of last night? I didn't mean to insult you. I will never do such a thing again. I will never ask about anything ever again."

Nefele squatted to her knees so she could be on eye level with him. She took his hands in hers and brought them to her lips. "I wish for you to have the world," she said. The words came out of her like a whisper, and at the same time a soft tingle ran all over her skin. Her earlier desire of wanting it "all to end" mingled with this new magic she unleashed, setting Simon free.

CHAPTER TWELVE

"What if all I want is to stay?"

Nefele closed her eyes and brought his fingers to her lips again. She kissed them softly, feeling the small hairs over his knuckles, smelling his sweat and loving it all. "You are married, Simon." His wife had been present in Nefele's thoughts, growing louder day by day as they continued to play husband and wife when Simon had an actual wife. Was it her parents that had instilled such respect for an institution that didn't matter, nor exist on the island? Or the books? The real world had become a fantasy land to her and she failed to distinguish its moral rules from her imaginations. "I can't keep you forever when you have a wife, that girl who loved you so much, can I? That wouldn't be fair."

She wanted to keep him. She wanted to silence all her worries, tell him the truth, share the diaries, the magic, and the island, and keep him. Tell him her name. But she also wanted him happy and the books forbade her from doing as she pleased. The island, with its secrets, its wonders and its magic, was a prison, and Simon was innocent.

"Fuck my wife," he snapped. "You are the witch. Why would you care about such things as marriage and my wife?"

"Because she must be filled with despair and fear over what happened to you when your ship returned and you were not on it. How could I ignore all that?"

"Because I can!" Simon grabbed the bed headboard and gripped it tightly as he squeezed his eyes shut. "I like it here."

His words should have elated Nefele. It was confirmation of all she wanted, it was the end she desired for their story, but the more his behaviour was a perfect reflection of her desires, the harder it was to accept them as truth. That flicker of magic, that direct link between her desires and him that had begun their current life was a barrier she couldn't tear down. What if all his accommodating nature, all the ways he had made her feel safe, were just the magic? What if the true Simon was buried beneath it, begging to be allowed to take control of his life again? What if she had stripped him of identity, like she had done with Auntie, and simply plastered over him this ideal dream?

"You don't know me," she whispered. "I am horrible. How can you want to stay here with me?"

Simon grabbed her head with his hands and kissed her. He bit her lips open, being forceful in his expression, unlike all their previous romantic moments, as his right hand moved through her hair and his left pulled her closer by the waist. Her entire body weight fell on her knees as he pulled her closer, forcing a painful scratching feeling. "I have done terrible things, too." He lost his balance, and pulled both of them aside into a tangled mess of limbs.

Nefele groaned from the graceless landing and shifted her body so she was sitting on her bottom, stretching her legs while she waited for the pain to ease. Simon leaned closer and offered her his hands but Nefele ignored him and kept on rubbing her knees.

"I really want to stay here. I am not innocent, like you think I am."

"Your crimes are a drop in the ocean compared to mine."

"You don't know that."

"I do," she insisted. "If you could commit the sins I have committed, they would have placed you on your own magical island."

He laughed at her words before leaning against the bed, making the entire furniture wobble. "I need to fix that."

Nefele placed her hand on his leg, stopping his small tests of the furniture's balance. "Just think about your future. Even if this vessel doesn't send boats here, another one will come and will. I will not be upset if you wish to leave. I will not hurt you. I will not place a curse on you or anything like that." She moved to get up but before she was able to manoeuvre her heels to press against the floor, Simon pulled her down.

"No. No more of this evading. At every chance of speaking, truly saying any kinds of truths, you run away. Enough! I want to stay."

"This island is a prison and you don't know what you want," Nefele said, attempting to reason with him.

"Stop talking to me like I am a child. I am a grown man

and I can make my own decisions. I want to stay and you just said that you wished for me to have anything I want. I wish to stay."

A myriad of excuses came to mind but Nefele didn't say any of them. "Why?" she asked him. "Why do you want to stay?" Her fear whispered that she was a fool for even contemplating that there was an ethical way for her not to be alone while her survival instincts rebelled against her desire, screaming their own protests that he had an ulterior motive and even his refusal to escape her was part of a secret plan.

His earlier emphasis on them continuing the conversation died. He stopped testing the durability of her bed and licked his lips, swollen and red at the edges from the kissing moments before. Had she broken the spell by asking the question? Wasn't the admittance of truth the greatest escape any soul could have? Even bitter ones offered relief when they were uncovered.

She sighed.

"I want to stay with you," he said, speaking slowly and carefully choosing each word, "because there is nowhere else on this earth that I wish to be."

"That's the same as what you said before," she challenged him. "Just worded differently. Why?" He climbed onto the bed, sitting on the side, and offered his hand to pull her up. Nefele accepted his help this time and they sat side by side. She focused on his bare feet instead of his face, thinking that they were so much bigger than hers. So much stronger. And paler. "I will answer your question, too," she promised, putting up a reward for his honesty. "Why you are different than those other people, like the pirates from the diary. But you must tell me first."

"I wish to be safe here with you, safe in the fairy tale and away from the rest of the world. I can just be Simon to you."

It was not the love declaration that she had read men speak in her romance books. His words offered her the relief of knowing she hadn't taken his will away, like she had done to Auntie. "Were you not just Simon to your family? Your wife?"

He shook his head. "In the world beyond the stories I read as a child, everything is messier. It is an easier life here. Being with you is the easiest thing I have ever experienced."

"Is it the witch you want? Or the woman?" She smiled at him, feeling older and wiser, even though she didn't have any right to claim either. She failed to remove bitterness from her voice when she asked her question, as well as her disappointment, because a tiny, hopeful and childish part of her wished for him to say he loved her. Nefele wished for her to love him as men and women did in the romance novels and in the fairytales that taught how love prevailed above all else.

She had become the witch out of myths and lived in a magical island that travelled all over the world, defying all rules of logic and fate. She had been allotted her share of fairy tales already.

"Tell me where the line between the witch and the woman is. Tell me so I can answer you."

This was her side of the bargain, the moment she wished for, she dreaded, and the end her magic was forcing to actualisation. "I am a witch," she whispered. "But not THE witch."

His lips parted as she bit her bottom lip and waited for his verdict. His eyes fluttered as he contemplated her words, reliving their entire time together under the prism of the new information. He brought his legs up on the bed, folding them in front of him while Nefele faced the floor and anticipated patiently his reaction to her months-long deception—the root of his entire imprisonment on the island, his months of starvation, his lost time—all to be rewarded by a fraud.

"Do you wish to leave the island then? *Can* you leave the island?"

Nefele shrugged. "I don't know. But I don't deserve to leave. I am as much its prisoner as the first witch."

"Then let's stay here, together." He squeezed her hands and she felt an unnatural heat coming from them. Was this magic, too? Had be bonded with the island enough for his desires to be honoured? When they were clear and precise, like the book explained they had to be? "I deserve a prison too. You know nothing about me. I am as guilty as you for more crimes."

"I created Auntie, Simon," Nefele admitted. "I am guilty of stripping the entire identity of a woman and sending her babies into the sea to drown." He wouldn't be able to forgive that, when Nefele couldn't do it. This revelation, above all others, would end all his wishing to stay with her. "I am a monster. I am a coward and selfish because I did this and couldn't even put them out of their misery. I kept them as a pet, to ease my loneliness." She wiped the new tears that formed in her eyes and brought her legs on the bed as well, hugging her knees and hiding her face between them. "So go back to your wife, Simon. If you even want to tell these sailors the truth, do it and send them my way. I do not mind."

"If I do that, the men who fly under that flag will rape you to death," Simon muttered.

In her mind Nefele had only imagined a bloody—but mostly quick—death at the hands of intruders, clinical and precise, terrible for signalling the end of her life but never prolonged and purposefully painful. The idea of sexual violence, always existing underneath the politically chosen abstract words of stories, had never entered her mind. "Maybe that's the death I deserve."

CHAPTER THIRTEEN

It was midday when he returned to the bedroom. Nefele had moved to the window, gazing at the ship which had been forced into stillness by the lack of wind. Too far for any of them to row to the island but close enough to see it and wonder why they had never located it in these waters before. Simon sat on the floor opposite her, stretching his legs over her own, and handed her a plate of food. "Eat," he ordered her.

She shook her head. "I am not hungry."

"Eat."

Too tired to fight, Nefele picked the plate and took the fork he gave her to stab into the stew they had prepared the previous day. She placed small doses of food into her mouth, chewing slowly and swallowing loudly half the portion he brought her. "I don't want anymore," she said when she gave up the food.

He nodded, took it off her, and began eating her leftovers. "I read some of the diaries. Auntie had placed them on your desk. Were you a castaway or abandoned to die here?"

"I was a castaway," Nefele admitted.

"How long have you been here?"

"It doesn't matter."

He squeezed her stretched-out calf. "It does to me. How old are you? How long have you been here? Tell me your story."

His firm grip over her loosened, and his hold turned into a soft caress that moved up and down her leg, reaching the middle of her thigh. "Why do you care about such things?"

His lips were soft when he discarded the plate at the side, moved forward, and kissed her forehead. "Because I hunger for all of you," he said, echoing her own words from a long time ago. "And above all, I crave your name."

"Nefele." She offered it and started laughing. "I haven't said it in nearly nine years."

His eyes blinked with surprise. "Nine years. Alone here? With only Auntie for company?"

Nefele shook her head. "Auntie has been here the last year and a half—or a bit more. I am not sure. It's easy to lose time when there are no clear seasons to depend on. I count the days but I often forget."

"And before that?"

"I had my elks."

"That's not enough," Simon said. "How old were you? How did you get here? How did you survive alone?"

"Leave it be, Simon. My story is not interesting and do not pity me, for I am made of such evil that I was impris- oned here before I had even committed the crime."

"Stop hiding from me. Stop evading the truth. I have had enough of it," he snapped, firmly taking her chin and forcing her to look at him. "Tell me. Tell me everything that happened to you, Nefele."

The sound of her name from his lips brought tears to her eyes because there hadn't been any memories of anyone speaking to her, Nefele, not the witch. She had banished them all, dirtied them with her wilful ignoring to extinction so she could be the witch and nothing else. "I came here when I was nine. Holding onto my father's corpse and wishing he could come back to life to help me because I was scared and lonely. And I stayed here because there was no other place to go and I played along because the diaries said I had to and because I was afraid of pirates and bad men. And I tried to forget my mother and father. My brother and sisters. I tried to forget my name. Until you came."

An irrational anger rose inside her, propelling her to place her palm against his chest and push him experimentally away.

"You came," she repeated and added more force behind her hand. "You arrived and stayed, destroying everything I had tried to become and creating a battlefield inside me. You, Simon, made me want things I had resigned to never having. You made my body my own enemy because I wanted you." She pushed him another time with further force and her throat ached from her raised voice.

"Do you not want me anymore?" Simon baited her.

She tried to pull her hand away, but he pressed it against his chest. "I cannot have you. I cannot keep you. The witch is always alone. The witch is always evil and cruel and unlovable and I am the witch because I have killed. I cannot stop being the witch now. The time for that has long passed. I cannot leave this island." His hold loosened and he released her. Nefele curled away from him, pressing her back against the window frame, trying to create any distance between them. "So go back to your wife, who loved you and wanted you, and you can have another baby and be happy."

"No," he said.

"Your wife is waiting," Nefele snapped at him. "She lost her baby and then she lost her husband because I, a villain, played stupid games and trapped you here."

"My wife and I lost our affections for one another before I boarded the merchant ship. You hold no responsibility over that." He had insinuated such a past, with Nefele's imagination adding details over their shared grief and the ghost of their dead child as to the reason behind their emotional distance.

"I have spent years trying to stop loving my family. And they still enter my dreams," she told him. "Do not tell me that you managed to banish her from your heart so easily."

He turned to look at the still sea, with the ship paused at the far horizon, unable to decide whether to approach them or to sail past them. "We are complicated creatures. You might not see that because you lost your childhood here, but lost love is very common." Before she could protest her own ignorance of human society, he added, "Books are fiction. They give you the most ideal version, whether that is pain or love, or even family. Art aims to smooth the edges in order to give you a compelling story. Real life is like a heap of discarded clothes, and you search amid them matching pieces for a narrative that will hold your sanity." He stood up and offered his hand to pull her up with him.

They left the room, with the half-eaten food still on the floor, and Simon guided Nefele to the kitchen, where a pile of diaries was assembled. "Auntie brings them down. I don't understand how they choose them. Have you read them all?"

Nefele nodded. "All the ones I have found in my mother tongue. I do not know any others."

Simon put a hand over her shoulders. "I do," he said.

"And you wish to stay to help me translate the stories of vile criminals?"

"I want to stay to escape the world out there, and everything I have done. Like all these women." He pointed at the diaries. "There is a reason this island chose me to stay with you. It understood that I had nowhere else to go, like them. Why does it matter so much that I am a man? Do you even know for certain that none of these accounts were written by a man? You assume that only women could find refuge here."

Could that be the answer? Could it be that she had misunderstood the truth of the word "witch", blinded by notions of her childhood? Words moved between languages, the island travelled between cultures, and none matched. "I do not know that for sure," she admitted. "But I do know this island is a prison."

He blinked at her twice and then his eyes narrowed with suspicion, the same way they did when he had caught her in a lie and contemplated whether he wished to press for the truth. She waited for whatever secret he thought he had unearthed to be spoken, eager to hear it, but the wind blew harshly against the glass, shaking the entire treehouse. Simon put his arms around Nefele and shielded her, waiting for the change of weather to pass. The initial gust of wind eased, although a strong blow endured, but the tree didn't waver against it anymore. Simon's eyes remained lit with suspicion and fragments of an understanding that escaped Nefele.

"The ship," he muttered and dashed to the ladder. Nefele trailed after him, like a duckling that didn't understand the world and only knew of their mother's wisdom as its sole guidance. Back at the top floor, Simon looked at the ship, which was now headed towards them, urged by the wind that directed it straight to the island. He nodded his head, as if he was agreeing with something that Nefele couldn't hear. "I think they will come exploring the island," he said. "I don't think we can hide away. Are there any more boxes you haven't gone through?"

Puzzled by his words, Nefele nodded and then shook her head, unsure as to what was the truth. "Maybe," she muttered.

"Where would they be?"

"Um," she tried to think. "Most were on the kitchen floor. There is the cellar, but that only has food. A few secret compartments on the floor." He grabbed her arm and pulled her.

"Let's go then."

He began emptying every box Nefele had found, with frantic urgency. "What are we looking for, Simon?" she asked and felt a jolt of apprehension at the use of the collective pronoun because just moments ago she had been trying to separate them.

"Binoculars. Or a telescope. Something to allow us to see with more detail who is coming. And how many."

She joined his search until, finally, he emptied a box and found a small coppery metal instrument that Nefele had never seen before. "There we go," he handed it to her. "Go upstairs and keep watch," he instructed. "I need to go set something outside. Lock the door," he said. "Do not approach them alone."

"I don't understand, Simon," she protested, feeling like all her years on the island had been invalidated by his assumption of control, making her feel the same as when she was nine and in need of a saviour.

"The fairytale is the answer, Nefele." Simon said each word between kisses. "We don't have time for more explanations now, so please trust me." She grabbed his arm and held him, trying to decide if she could allow him to do as he pleased on her island. Clinging to him, she embraced his waist. "Can you trust me?" he asked.

Could she? Did she want to? Nefele had never been brave. Even from her few remaining glimpses of her childhood, she understood that she had never been the exploring kind of child. In her childish games, she had followed Fanouris or her little sister, Maria, who paved the way and urged her to follow. "Yes," she muttered, not sure if this was the truth but wishing for it to be so more than she cared to contemplate.

"Go, then, and keep watch. I will be back soon." He turned back after a few steps towards the door. "Lock it."

* * *

The ship lowered two boats and Nefele counted three men on each one rowing towards the island. They all wore similar clothes to those Simon wore when he first arrived, the generic sailor clothes as she branded them, and they reached the shore by nightfall. She heard the elks' distinctive cries and moved to the bottom floor. There was no need to keep watch anymore.

The door banged and she jumped in fright before she remembered that the island was too vast for any of them to have reached the treehouse, especially when they didn't know the way to it amid the trees. She moved the door tentatively, fearing each sound she made, and pressed her head to the door. "Simon?" she whispered.

"It's me," he replied and she unlatched the door. "This is the plan," he said when he came inside.

* * *

Nefele's original ideas of dealing with intruders only using the sheer force of the myth as a weapon were naïve and childish. She hadn't paid enough attention to the right diaries, and that could have been her undoing. The island, though, needs a prisoner and will do all it can to ensure its witch survives.

* * *

Nefele rode her elk friend to the lake, where she met three of the six sailors. "Why are you on my island?" she asked, looking down on them.

The three men had lit a fire, which allowed them to

pinpoint her location quickly. The flame danced as it consumed the dry leaves and logs they had given it as fuel, making the shadows over the sailor's faces move around their features and them look more menacing than she suspected they were under daylight. "This is no one's island," one of them said, in a clipped accent, and stood up, dusting off his clothes. "We are scavenging the waters, by the order of King Faustian. From the moment we came here, this island is his. Who are you?"

Nefele took a deep breath and willed herself to continue the fairytale, to play the witch as she had done before. "This is my island," she said. "And I have no King, nor Queen, to order me to surrender it. I recognise no authority and no power but my own. Even the Gods feared me so greatly that they had to trap me here." The words rolled easily through her mouth, practiced lines and sentiments uttered from hundreds of women before her, all playing the same role.

Two of them burst out laughing. "What is this?" one of them spoke between his laughter. "Are you the famed enchantress, the walking gorgon?"

"Is that how you know of me?" Nefele asked, taking the lead from his words that the fairytale they referred to matched her own. It mattered little after all, whether the island was the source of it or not. "I demand you leave my island. This is the only way to save your lives."

One of them, a middle-aged man with a crooked nose, seemed to not understand a word she said and panic filled her because she wished for them to take her offer and leave, avoiding the need to spill their blood and ensuring both her and Simon would remain safe, since he refused to leave alongside them. The third man, a handsome blonde, looked uncertain, his eyes glancing between his bravado-filled comrade and her. He leaned in and whispered in a language Nefele didn't comprehend. The third man laughed nervously but still made an involuntary movement, clutching his shirt and spitting inside it.

"Listen, girl, I do not know what kind of madness possesses you but we can help you," he said. He approached and offered his hand. "We can take you with us, make you a real woman, save you from the wilderness."

"I have no need to be saved. All I ask is for you to leave my home and return to your ship. Do you refuse?"

The other two men stood up as well. Nefele looked at the handsome blonde and raised her eyebrow towards him, although she wasn't sure if her facial expressions were easily distinguishable under the faint illumination of the fire. "Translate to your friend. I do not wish him to die because he doesn't understand the language."

"If anyone is going to die tonight, that will be you," the first man said, shorter than the other two, and folded his arms, exposing a tattoo. "But I do not wish for your death. Surrender and we will save you."

Nefele ignored him. "Translate," she demanded of the blonde. She pointed towards the west, "If you go that way, you will reach a rocky beach and if you turn to the left, you should find your boats eventually." She waited until the blonde man whispered what she said.

"Sven," the man snapped and then spoke in the same tongue they did.

"If you run towards the beach, I will not chase you and allow you time to leave. If you run towards me, you will die," she said.

Sven, the blonde man, whispered while she spoke. The third man, with the crooked nose, nodded in understanding and Nefele saw him slowly retreat, walking backwards and taking the offer of life that Nefele gave him. Her heart beat fast against her chest, urging both of the other men to do as she wanted and for their altercation to end quickly.

The crooked man turned around and ran. "Sab!" Sven froze, unsure how to decide, and Nefele sympathised with him because she had frozen in crossroads before and had needed an external push to find a way forward. She cleared her mind of all thoughts and all other feelings and wished, with her own benefit as the focus, that Sven would follow Sab and flee. The gulp she recognised as magic made her twitch slightly and Sven ran.

The first man stayed still and spat on the ground. "You are a good actress," he praised her. "But I am not easily fooled." He let out a loud yell and ran towards her.

In the timespan that took him to take three long dashes towards her and the elk, Nefele closed her eyes and a new soft jolt of magic went through her, killing the flames and engulfing the world in darkness, save some soft rays of moonlight that escaped the clouds and reflected on the body of water.

"Chase me, then," Nefele baited him and she softly nudged her elk to ride away.

CHAPTER FOURTEEN

The man yelled in his native language and Nefele heard him running after her. She held onto the elk's large and elaborate antlers, controlling their speed so the man wasn't left too far behind. Simon's plan depended upon none of the sailors remaining alive on the island. She hadn't asked him why, neither did she wish to find out what he would do if they failed and someone did roam the island alongside them. Nefele only knew that she didn't wish for another experience like the one she had initially had with Simon, fearing walking around her home and not sure if she was being secretly watched.

"You can still go back," she suggested to him, but her offer was rejected with a growl. She took the long way around the forest, avoiding the treehouse as she led the man to the sunken garden, where Simon had told her to go. There were three more sailors somewhere on the island and she wondered if Simon had found them or if they had found him. She shook her head. Simon had warned her they might separate and assured her there was no need to worry about that.

She approached the area where the garden was but stopped the elk when she saw Simon tied to a tree and, where the sunken area was supposed to be, there were leaves. She squinted her eyes and realised that multiple branches had been placed between the ground and the pillars but, given the low visibility of the night, it was hard to distinguish the difference. If she hadn't known what to expect, Nefele would have been easily fooled. The elk walked with confidence around the area and turned to face the sailor who was running behind them.

"Simon?" she said.

"Trust me," he whispered and then relaxed his face before assuming an expression of anguish, and tears rolled down his face.

The sailor who chased her finally crossed the last few trees and entered the clearing where the sunken garden was hidden. Simon let out a scream, startling Nefele before she remembered the role she had to play, and she hid her surprise with an expression of aloof indifference. The sailor paused, breathing hard and holding himself up by gripping onto the bark of the closest trunk. His eyes needed a moment to adjust before he noticed Simon. His angry expression faded into one of confusion. Before he could do anything else, Simon began thrashing against the trunk, restrained by the rope he had around his body. "Run," he yelled. "She will make you her prisoner. Run!" He spoke in other languages—Nefele recognised the different intonations as he switched.

"What is this?" the sailor asked in his clipped accent, emphasising all his Ts and Ss.

"Run," Simon repeated. "Please go! If you don't have a boat, swim away," he cried and let out a deep throat wail that Nefele had never heard anyone make. "It is better than staying here." The sailor's earlier bravado completely faded as he assessed the new situation.

"You can still save yourself," Nefele reminded him. She pointed to the south. "There is a beach there, just walk around the edge of the island until you find your comrades and then return to your ship and sail away, never mentioning that you found this island."

The sailor hesitated and Nefele felt the tug of her earlier magic, wishing for him, along with Sven and Sab, the other two sailors she had found him with, to flee.

"Please go," Simon cried. "Please."

"But," the sailor protested and tried to step forward.

"No," Simon stopped him again. "I cannot leave with you but you can escape. You don't have much time left."

The sailor turned to Nefele. "What is this? Who are you?"

For a moment she forgot who she ought to be, confused as to what she could say to explain what the sailor was seeing and still convince him to leave. Her heart beat in her chest and the chill of the night made the hair over her hands rise and, if she was standing, her knees would shake. "I am the witch," she said. "This is my island and you are trespassing. If you take any more steps towards us, you will die. Your family will never learn what happened to you."

The man shook his head.

"They will not come to save you," Nefele said, because that never happened in the diaries. Nobody ever sent reinforcements for the lost sailors or castaways. The island moved away once the fate of its intruders was decided, faster than any ship could follow. "You know of me," she pressed, hoping that he would have heard of at least one story she could play against him. "This island is a prison," she said, breaking away from the character of the witch for a moment.

The sailor didn't move.

"If the rest of them," Simon said, moving his head towards the elk she rode on, "arrive, it will be too late for you."

"But you," he protested, and Nefele felt a knot form in her throat at the idea of kindness being the cause of his death. Why wasn't he listening?!

"Save yourself," Simon urged him. "Go!"

The sailor looked behind him, and it seemed he was waiting for something else to happen, another answer to be given to him. "I am tasked by King Faustian to be here," he said. "This island belonged to him from the moment I stepped on it, because my body carries his will and I will honour my king and his God-ordained mission to understand the world."

"Then you will die," Nefele said.

"Listen to her," Simon insisted. There was a loud cry from the elks that shook the entire island. "This island cannot be conquered, and you will run out of time," he warned the man, the urgency dripping from his tongue.

There was another loud elk scream and the sound of soft steps from behind him made the sailor jump, landing right at the edge of where the sunken garden lay. One step, one small push, and he would be gone. He yelled in his own language and then, "Who is there? What is this place?"

After a moment, Auntie walked past the final shade of darkness, wearing the green dress that Nefele had worn on the day that they arrived on the island, when they had a will and life of their own. The sailor let out a yelp but stood still. Nefele's breath caught in her throat as she waited to see what would happen. "Devil!"

"Run," she whispered under her breath, hoping that her magic would make him move forward and that there would still be a boat waiting for him on the shore.

Auntie walked towards him; the sailor backed away. Nefele closed her eyes as she heard wood snapping, a surprised yelp, and then the loud thump of someone landing. When she opened her eyes again, Simon had escaped the rope around his body while more elks, including the female cow who had taken to acting as Auntie's protector and carer, appeared amid the trees. Their eyes glowed in the dark, looking like devils, and they all stared at her.

"Five out of six," Simon muttered. He approached the edge, where he went on his knees and looked down at the man. "You should have listened to us."

Whatever response the sailor said, Nefele didn't hear, or it was spoken in a language she couldn't understand while Simon replied back in it. She waited for Simon to translate but the entire conversation between the two men remained a mystery to her.

* * *

Anyone's imagination can fill the blanks as to what was said. Nefele, after she ate and slept, did the same. There wasn't much to be said to a soon-to-be-dead man.

* * *

Auntie took Nefele's hand and guided her back to the treehouse. They led her to the yellow velvet couch, and sat by her side, holding her hand. "Auntie," she muttered. She wet her lips to try and speak any kind of truth between them but found it hard to express how sorry she was that she had dragged them into the darkness. "I wish I had been kinder to you," she whispered. She was sorry, not for taking their gender—or not simply that. Her guilt danced around the concept of choice and freedom, all which she had removed by force. If it had only been a physical change, although cruel and unfair, Nefele didn't think she would feel such self-hatred each time she gazed at Auntie—if it had only been breasts that she had taken, not Auntie's entire identity.

* * *

It was for this reason that Nefele could never receive absolution for that first crime. There wasn't much of Auntie left to be able to forgive all Nefele did, if the woman they once were ever would.

* * *

Simon returned by dawn and woke Nefele with a kiss on the cheek. "You should go to bed," he suggested but she shook her head, wiping her sleep tears and the eye-gum that had crusted over her lashes. "It's done," he said and kissed her forehead.

"He's dead?" she asked, even though she knew the answer.

Simon kissed her forehead again and caressed her hair. "I wished we could have convinced all of them to flee. But five out of six is a good outcome. I went to the beach and watched the ship disappear. I am not sure if they moved away or we did, but the danger has passed."

"Why did you do this?" she asked him. The idea of his hands soaked with blood, carrying the responsibility of having stolen a life, made her choke.

"Hey, hey," he cooed at her. "I told you, Nefele, I have done my share of sins." He showed her his hands, brown from dirt. "I think I understand this island. I think I have the final piece. Magic is desire, right?"

Nefele didn't remember ever telling him that and a part of her old fear that she knew so little about Simon resurfaced but another, calmer and more resigned piece of her whispered that all would be well. Because, after all that had happened, why would one more inconsistency in their story matter? She nodded.

"It was the Gods—or whoever the original jailor was— who trapped the first witch. Their desire makes the island a prison. But the witch had magic of her own. She couldn't alter the desire of the jailor, already in play, but her own wants became magic and turned this island into a home for her. The two desires fought and eventually merged. Do you see, Nefele?"

She didn't. Simon understood her inability to follow his thoughts and sighed before he sat next to her. "The fairytale is the answer, I told you before. The fairytale is the trap. The island became myth and a folk story so both desires could be honoured. It lures women—or men," he added in haste, "who are guilty so it can keep a prisoner. But then the island keeps them alive, so it could also be haven and home. And that is why nothing about it makes sense."

Her mind struggled to see the full picture that Simon had painted for her. She didn't wish to think of it in such terms, that all the wonders, all the joys, were both trap and relief, and yet it fit the narrative she had read a hundred times over, whether the women—or men—had been trapped by others or had fled to avoid the world. "But why me, then?" she asked him. "Why would I end up here? What had I done?"

"What if it didn't lure you," he suggested softly, "but your father? However, you were the only one who survived?"

"My father was a good man," she protested, like a child defending her parents, because she loved her father, who had been kind to her and offered her safety.

"He might have been kind-hearted to you," Simon whispered. "But others might not agree. He might have felt guilty for leaving the rest of his family behind. Why did you travel alone? Where were your mother and siblings? Your story didn't begin on a boat, Nefele."

There was a pain in her head, like she had been smacked with wood and had a concussion. The image of falling from a tree flashed. He took her hand in his and began massaging it. "Whether it was you or him, or it was just bad luck, it doesn't matter. That is one thing all the diaries seem to agree on: how you arrived doesn't matter. Your life starts anew on this island. Which always has a full cellar, and a freshwater lake, despite its size, but all the magic in the world is not enough to stop you from having to work the land hard, scavenge, and go to bed tired each night. This prison island found itself occupied by a little girl, who didn't understand the world, with no parental guidance, and who wanted fairy tales to be real. What kind of person would you grow up to be, if all your instructions were the words of lonely, long-lost people, most of whom certainly were violent and cruel? You reflect the prisoners the island needs to hold."

"Why would you stay here, then?" she asked.

"Who wouldn't prefer the simplicity of fairytales, over the complexity of reality?" he asked instead of answering.

* * *

It took Nefele years to accept that answer, but she was grateful for the explanation. She spent many nights tossing around in bed until she found an excuse to all that plagued her mind under the shield of the fairytale trap.

CHAPTER FIFTEEN

They didn't discuss the sailor incident. Days later, Nefele woke up alone in their bed. She searched the house and found Simon in the kitchen, sitting at the table, with Auntie at his side. "What are you doing?"

He lifted a piece of paper on which she recognised his handwriting. "I started my own diary."

The idea that his story would survive alongside hers stung for a moment, but she pushed the discomfort aside, because Simon was as much the witch as she was.

* * *

In the end, perhaps we became the witch together. Two sides of the same idea. Her the castaway who never left and me, a criminal who hid in a magical prison.

* * *

She leaned over his shoulders, reading his words, narrating their encounter with the sailor. "Was it that easy with the other three?" He nodded.

"One look at Auntie and they turned. I think they are our greatest shield."

She kissed his cheek and then Auntie's head, caressing their hair and embracing them tightly. Nefele tried to wish to restore them to who they once were, or even to return to them a part of their identity. There was no jolt, no sensation to signify that any part of her desire turned into magic, for she didn't sincerely wish for Auntie to return to their old self, despite how sorry she was for transforming the mother into the beloved creature in her arms.

"When the next ship comes, you can still take your leave," she suggested as she stared at the stained-glass women.

His writing stopped. "And if I wish to stay?"

"Then you must continue the fairytale."

He laughed and moved to stand behind her, putting his arms around her waist and kissing her neck. Nefele closed her eyes and sighed, until Auntie got up, their chair tipping to the side as they moved away from the kitchen area to the ugly yellow sofa.

His kisses remained sweet and their relationship grew to true companionship as the years passed, but he never told her about his past, his wife's name. Nor the baby's.

* * *

They remained, like in fairy stories, nameless characters, part of an intangible past that mattered little. After all, how often in the original fairy tales—not the retellings so beloved—do you ever know a dead mother's name?

* * *

It was all about the fairy tale, not the truth.

ACKNOWLEDGMENTS

The Castaway and the Witch began its life as a short story in 2021. It was an experiment on crafting a narrative which extensively used the literary device of foreshadowing and writing a negative character arc. It was only a little over 4,000 words and narrated a simplified version of the first three chapters of this novella.

After many unsuccessful attempts to publish it as a short story, in 2023, I decided to expand it, primarily because I felt that the bare worldbuilding was the reason behind my difficulty in finding it a home. The idea of Simon was born at that time, but I didn't really plan to write him into this extended new version. Instead, I focused on exploring the mythos behind the island and the Floating Forest as a space. I poured into it all my favourite elements of fairytale scenery (although some didn't make the final cut)! In this second iteration, the story turned into a novel-ette of about 11,000 words. It was in this version that the idea of writing the Floating Forest as a reimagining of Aeaea, Circe's island from Greek mythology, first emerged.

In 2024 I found myself very stuck creatively. I was writing a hybrid elevated horror/gothic novel which progressed slowly and was very painful. I also went through a harsh episode of imposter syndrome and writer's block which led me to rereading a lot of my older pieces, especially unpublished ones. It was through this that I decided to return, once again, to this story and explore this Simon fellow which I had first thought of in the 2023 rewrite. It was such a refreshing feeling of relief to add to this story again, to explore within it Nefele's life beyond her failed attempt to become the Witch. It turned into this nearly cerebral novella which I see as filled with allegories about morality, and the role of fiction within reality. Very much like Simon, I have often wished to escape the world I live in and dive into a fairytale or, more often, the world of a sitcom where certain status quo elements never change. I delved into that intense desire for escapism and the story flew out of me and it became the tale that you read and hopefully enjoyed.

Like my debut novel, The Castaway and The Witch wouldn't have been written without the help and support of many people who surround me in life. Firstly, I would like to thank my publisher, Antonia Rachel Ward, for believing in this story and being willing to publish it, even though it was a bit of departure from my previous work. I always joke that my writing is unpublishable, and I am so glad you were willing to give this piece a chance.

Ed Crocker, my editor, deserves a huge thank you for the meticulous work he put in improving the novella. I know the story would have been far uglier without your keen eye and my anxiety would have skyrocketed without your patient replies over minute details of the story.

Thank you to everyone who has read my work until now. I am amazed that anyone finds what I have to say interesting, and I am so grateful that we have found each other! I also want to thank everyone in the Edinburgh SFF community and the British Fantasy Society. Thank you for providing safe spaces to learn from fellow authors and make new connections within the writing world. Thank you to Danai Christopoulou who has always been one of the most supportive voices online for all authors! I always value and respect your input into the publishing world. Thank you, Sophia-Maria Nicolopoulos, for always supporting my work.

Thank you, Marialena, for not mincing your words when you read the original short story. I am not sure if the novella would have been written without your input in its novelette stage.

Thank you to my dear friend Glyka! You have been a treasured addition to my life and one of the people whose opinion on writing and books I trust the most. Thank you for always being willing to read my work. Without a doubt, you offer me the most detailed and thought-provoking reviews! My writing – and my life – has exponentially improved thanks to you!

I am always grateful to my family who never stop believing in me. A special mention to my sister, Alexandra, who is one of my greatest cheerleaders in life!

Finally, last but by no means least, I wouldn't have written this book without my husband. Kavan, thank you for putting up with all the nonsense I come up with on a daily basis and for still being willing to write with me every day. Thank you for always listening and always calming my anxieties so I can continue trying.

ABOUT THE AUTHOR

IOANNA PAPADOPOULOU is a Greek fantasy and speculative fiction author, based in Scotland. Other than writing, she is passionate about art history and museology. Her debut novel, *Winter Harvest*, was published by Ghost Orchid Press in November 2023.

ALSO BY IOANNA PAPADOPOULOU

Winter Harvest

www.ingramcontent.com/pod-product-compliance
Lightning Source LLC
Chambersburg PA
CBHW010319100726
47906CB00006B/1056